RIDING
STORIES

KINGFISHER
An imprint of Kingfisher Publications Plc
New Penderel House, 283-288 High Holborn
London WC1V 7HZ
www.kingfisherpub.com

This edition first published by Kingfisher 2005
2 4 6 8 10 9 7 5 3 1
Originally published as *Thundering Hooves* by Kingfisher 1996
Published as *More Horse and Pony Stories* by Kingfisher 1998

A CIP catalogue record for this book is available from the British Library

ISBN-13: 978 0 7534 1151 3
ISBN-10: 0 7534 1151 2
1TR/THOM/MAR/80NS/F

Printed in India

RIDING
STORIES

CHOSEN BY
CHRISTINE PULLEIN-THOMPSON

ILLUSTRATED BY
VICTOR AMBRUS

KINGFISHER

CONTENTS

THE WHITE MUSTANG

EDWARD McCOURT

T HE BOY HAD RUN all the way from the upland pasture and his thin eager face was damp with sweat. His father was standing at the shady end of the barn sharpening a mower knife, and the grating noise of granite drawn over steel sounded loud in the afternoon stillness. The boy stopped directly in front of his father, shoved his hands deep into the pockets of his faded blue denim overalls and spat in the dust that lay thick around his bare feet. Some saliva dribbled over his chin and he quickly wiped it away with the back of his hand, hoping that his father had not noticed. "Dad – what do you think I saw way up on the Hog's-Back?"

His father held the mower knife upright and began methodically testing the triangular blades with his thumb. "What, Jed?"

"A horse – a grey horse! I figger maybe it's the one the Judsons lost and Mr Judson said he'd give five dollars reward to anyone who found him! Gee, Dad, can't I ride up and see? If I got the five dollars I'd be able to send for the twenty-two in the catalogue. It only costs six thirty-five

7

delivered and I've got a dollar and a half now."

The words burst out with a kind of explosive force that left the boy breathless and red in the face. He inhaled deeply, making a sucking noise, and scuffed the dirt with his bare feet. His father picked up the sharpening stone and eyed it critically.

"Not today, son," he said. "It's a long way up to the Hog's-Back on a hot day like this."

Jed turned away and looked at the big poplars down by the creek and tried not to think of anything at all. "But maybe tomorrow," his father said. "You could start right after breakfast. Only – "

"Gee, Dad – that'll be great! I could be back for dinner easy."

"Only you see, Jed, I can't figure how Judson's horse could have got up to the Hog's Back. Not from their side anyway. It's a mighty steep climb and there's no grass to lead a horse on. You're sure you saw one up top?"

"Gee, yes, Dad, just as plain as anything – standing right on the skyline. Honest it was a horse. Grey, nearly white I guess, just like the Judsons'. I was 'bout half a mile up in the pasture picking strawberries when I saw him."

His father leaned the mower-knife against the wall of the barn. As if a cord holding them in place had suddenly given away, his long limbs relaxed and he collapsed on the ground, his back miraculously against the wall of the barn, his legs straight out in front of him. From his overalls' pocket he pulled out a blackened pipe, held it between thumb and forefinger and looked at it without saying anything. Then his eyes crinkled at the corners.

"Son, I don't figure that was the Judson horse you saw at all."

Jed knew that his father was playing a game. Dermot O'Donnell loved to play games. Jed laughed out loud and sprawled in the dust at his father's feet. "Then whose horse was it?"

"No one's, Jed. You've seen the white mustang."

8

"What white mustang, Dad?"

Dermot's heavy eyebrows shot up and threatened to disappear into his hair-line. "Child, child, what do they teach you in school anyway. Nothing that matters or you'd have heard of the white mustang!"

He tamped down the tobacco in his pipe and struck a match along the leg of his overalls, all the time wagging his head slowly from side to side. "There's hardly a puncher in the plains country clear from the Rio Grande to Calgary who hasn't seen the white mustang at one time or another. Mostly at night of course, when the moon is shining and he looks more silver than white. You can get closer to him too, but not very close at that. But sometimes they see him in the daytime, only away off, and he doesn't stand long then."

"And has nobody ever caught him?"

"Not yet, Jed. You see, he's no ordinary horse. Seems like he never gets any older. And some fools have shot at him, but they either missed or the bullets went right through him and did no hurt at all. Anyway, no one has ever even slowed him up. And you can't catch him on horseback. Once, so they tell me, they took after him in relays – down in the Texas Panhandle it was – and chased him three days without a stop. But the white mustang never turned a hair. At the end of the three days two horses were dead and a lot more windbroken for life. But they never got within half a mile of the mustang and every so often he'd turn round and laugh at them the way a horse does if he's feeling extra good. Last I heard he was down in Wyoming working north. Way I figure it, no ordinary horse could get up the Hog's-Back from the Judson side. I guess it's the white mustang all right."

"Will you give me five dollars if I catch him?"

"Five dollars is it? Five dollars?" The pain in Dermot's voice was almost real. "Jed, if ever you catch the white mustang, you'll find him tame as a turtle-dove. And when you get on his back he'll take you away – just like flying it'll be, I think – to a country you've never seen where the grass is as green as the spring feathers of a mallard. And in a little glen so close to the sea you can hear the waves wash on the rocks, you'll find a beautiful princess with long golden hair waiting for you. And she'll get up behind you and put her arms around your middle and the white mustang will bring you back like he's a flash of lightning. And I'll build a house for you and the princess in the poplars down by the creek, and the two of you will be able to help your mother and me. And all your children – you'll have a grand houseful of them in no time – will learn to ride on the back of the white mustang, and when their time comes they'll ride away on him to be kings and queens all over the world. But mind you, Jed, no one has ever yet laid a rope on the white mustang."

Jed spoke thoughtfully. "I think I'd sooner have five dollars."

Jed's father was the most wonderful man in the world and his laughter was the most wonderful part of him. He laughed now, silently at first, then in a series of staccato explosions that culminated in a sustained gargantuan bellow. Jed laughed too; he always did, listening to his father. Then he ran away and lay down on his back in the middle of the grove of poplars where his father was going to build the house for the princess, and looked up through the tree-tops at the blue sky and thought of the things he would do with the twenty-two rifle.

Jed did not ride up to the Hogs'-Back the next day. For the heat-wave broke in a drenching rain that began as a thunderstorm over the mountains and spread out across the foothills in a steady, settled downpour. Jed tried not to show his disappointment. He knew that the rain was needed badly, that without it his father's small crop, already stunted and parched and clinging precariously to life, would have been burnt beyond hope of recovery in a week or less. But such considerations were of the theoretic and remote, of small weight beside the immediate loss of a day's adventure and five dollars at the end of it.

Late in the afternoon Jed put on the high rubber boots and oil slicker which were among his most prized possessions and climbed up the path through the pasture and beyond until he was no more than a mile from the Hog's-Back, an immense arching hill-top that seemed as remote as a mountain-peak and almost as inaccessible. There was not path beyond the fenced upland pasture, and the long slope above was steep and treacherous underfoot. Jed had been up to the Hog-s-Back only once; his father had taken him there one cool spring day, and the memory of what he had seen from the summit was like a lovely haunting dream. Now that he had been granted permission to go alone, the delay seemed to eat at his stomach and leave a hollow ache unlike any other pain he had ever known. Once, when he looked up, the swirling mists far up the slope seemed to part for a moment, and he glimpsed a whiteness that was no part of the elements. It was a whiteness that you didn't see in horses very often, and its outlines, vague and indistinct though they were, suggested the existence of something strange and portentous behind the wavering curtain of mist. Then the clouds closed in again and there were no more breaks. At last, when the rain had penetrated his slicker at a dozen points and was running in cold rivulets down his back, Jed turned away and half-walked, half-slithered down through a tangle of undergrowth to the comparative level of the pasture below.

He was quiet at supper that night. His mother had made his favourite dish of beef stew with puffy white dumplings floating in the gravy, and for a while there was no time to talk. But when the dessert came – pie made of dried apples and Saskatoon berries – Jed stopped with the first mouthful impaled on his fork and looked at his father. "Dad, is the white mustang very big?"

Dermot chewed a mouthful of food and swallowed. "Not big, Jed. A mustang is never big. But he looks big – like everything that's uncommon. Take Napoleon now. You'd measure him for a uniform and he was a small man, a runt – not much over five feet, I guess. And then you'd stand back and look at him and he was big. He was the biggest man you ever saw." That was another thing about Dermot – he made you feel that he had known Napoleon very well in the old days. Or Robin Hood or Brian Boru, or whoever he happened to be talking about.

Jed's mother filled Dermot's cup to the brim with strong black tea.

"What nonsense are you stuffing the boy's head with now, Dermot?" she asked. She was a small frail woman, the physical antithesis of her husband. But there was the same look in her dark eyes, a kind of remoteness in them that made her concern for the immediate seem casual at best.

"No nonsense, Mother, no nonsense at all. He hears enough of that at school."

"I wouldn't say that in front of the boy, Dermot," she said. "Maybe he'll learn enough at school to help him keep

one foot on the solid earth. Dear knows it's more than he'll
ever learn at home."

But she spoke without malice. And she looked at Dermot
and Jed in a way that seemed to make no difference
between them.

Next morning the sun shone from a clear sky and the
mists rose from the earth in steaming exhalations that
vanished before the cool wind blowing from the north-
west. The ground underfoot was soft and spongy – muddy
where there was no grass – and the grass itself washed
clean of dust so that it looked as if it had turned green
again overnight. Jed dressed quickly and hurried into the
kitchen for breakfast. "It's a swell day, Dad," he said.

His father set a pail full of milk on the shelf in the little
pantry adjoining the kitchen. "A fine day indeed, Jed. And
I know what's in your mind. But I'll have to take Paddy
and ride out to the far pasture this morning to look for the
yearlings. They didn't come up with the cows and I'm
thinking the fence may be down. But you'll be able to make
the Hog's-Back this afternoon. It'll be a cool day I think."

Jed did not protest about the delay. He knew what his
father was thinking, that the grey horse would be gone
anyway and that half a day would make no difference. He
swallowed the lump in his throat and ate breakfast quietly
but without appetite. After breakfast, when Dermot had
ridden off down the valley to the far pasture in the flats, he
amused himself snaring gophers in the little patch of wheat
just across the creek. But it was not a pastime that he ever
really enjoyed. He got a thrill from seeing the grey-brown
head pop up from the hole in the earth – from the quick
savage pull that trapped the victim – from the feel of
weight at the end of the long line of binder-twine as he
swung it through the air. But what had to be done
afterwards was not so pleasant. Particularly he hated
taking the string from the neck of the battered carcass,
covered with blood and insides as it so often was. This
morning his attempts were half-hearted and mostly

unsuccessful. After a while he threw his string away and returned to the house. He felt hungry, and there were cookies in the big green tin on the bottom shelf of the cupboard, and milk in the earthenware jug that always stood in the coolness of the cellar steps. He poured out a cup of milk, sat down at the table and ate his way steadily through a plateful of cookies. His mother was busy at the small work-table by the window. Jed finished his last mouthful of cookie and pushed back his chair.

"Mom?"

"What is it, Jed?"

"Mom, did you ever hear about the white mustang?"

"Only what your father told you." Mrs O'Donnell lifted a pie from the oven, using a corner of her ample gingham apron to protect her hands from the heat, and set it on the work-table. She stood beside the table looking out of the window, and her voice was so low that Jed could hardly hear her.

"Your grandmother used to tell me a story about a white horse. The son of Finn rode way on him to fairyland where he lived with a beautiful princess. They called her Naim the Golden-haired. But he got lonely and rode back on the white horse to his own country. He knew that he shouldn't get off the white horse, but he wanted to feel the turf under his feet. And the white horse ran away and the son of Finn turned into an old man. That's what happens to people when they come back to earth."

Jed emptied his cup and set it on the table. "It's a funny thing, Mom. An awful lot of people believe in the white horse, don't' they?"

His mother turned from the window without speaking. After a while Jed went back outside. He walked part way up the path to the pasture, then cut across to where the creek, rising from a spring far up in the hills, ran over rocks and gravel to the valley below. He sat on a flat rock and let the water trickle over his bare feet. The water was cold, but he liked the sensation of numbness stealing through his feet – first the instep, then the toes, heels last of all. Even better he liked the pricking feel of returning warmth when he drew his feet out of the water and warmed them on the surface of the rock. He stayed there for a long time, until he heard his mother's high "coo-ee" and knew that it was time for dinner.

Dermot was late getting home. So late that Mrs O'Donnell put his dinner away in the warming oven of the big range and brewed a fresh pot of tea. Jed waited stoically; but when he saw his father approaching up the valley trail he shouted at the top of his lungs and ran down to open the gate for him.

"Gee, Dad, I thought you were never going to get here!"

Dermot slid down from the saddle and stretched prodigiously.

"It was just as I thought – fence down and the yearlings miles away. Paddy has had a hard morning."

"He's too fat," Jed said. "He'll be all right in a little while."

He emptied a tin pail of oats into the manger feed-box while Dermot unsaddled the sweating pony. They went into the house together without saying anything. Mrs O'Donnell was setting Dermot's dinner on the table. "You're late, Dermot," she said.

"I am late, Mother. And I'm thinking it would be as well if Jed waited till morning now. Paddy needs a couple of hours' rest at least. And the grey horse is sure to be far away by this time."

Mrs O'Donnell spoke with unusual sharpness. "Paddy can have his rest and there still will be plenty of time. The evenings are long and the boy will be home before dark."

Jed's heart gave a great leap. His father grinned at him. "And they tell you it's the women-folk are over-anxious about their young," was all he said.

It was after two o'clock when Jed went to the barn to saddle Paddy. He threw the heavy stock-saddle over

Paddy's broad back and pulled the cinch tight. There was quite a trick to tightening the cinch. You had to pretend you were all finished so that the little sorrel would relax his distended belly. Then you gave the cinch-strap a quick sharp pull and took in about three inches of slack. As soon as the saddle was securely in place Jed shortened the stirrups and tied a lasso to the cantle. He could not throw a lasso very well, and anyway the Judson horse was a quiet nag that could be led on a halter-shank. But the lasso looked impressive, and it was a good idea always to be ready for anything.

He rode Paddy to the water-trough and let him drink a few mouthfuls. His mother came to the door and he waved to her and she waved back and smiled. "Don't be late, Jed."

"I won't," he shouted. "So long, Mom!"

For nearly an hour he rode upwards without pause, the pony stumbling often in the damp uncertain footing. The valley slid farther and farther away below him until at last Jed was able to see over the opposite side to the great plain itself. He stopped at last, not because he wanted to, but Paddy was blowing heavily. He dropped to the ground and squatted on his haunches while Paddy stood quietly beside him with bowed head. Jed could no longer see his own house because of an intervening swell in the seemingly regular contour of the hillside, but other houses had come into view – Joe Palamiro's shack near where the valley ran out into the plain, and the Peterson place, easily identified because of the big windmill, right at the edge of the plain itself. And he could see, far out on the plain, a row of tall gaunt red buildings – grain elevators – standing like guardsmen on parade, and beyond them a second row, over the horizon itself, so that only the upper halves of the elevators were visible. Another time Jed would have been tempted to linger, trying to identify familiar landmarks when seen from an unfamiliar angle. But now, after only a minute or two, he stirred restlessly. Paddy tossed his head and began to nibble at a few tufts of grass growing around the base of a boulder. Jed leapt to his feet.

"All right, you old geezer," he said. "If you can eat you can travel. I'll lead you for a while."

He unfastened the halter-shank from the saddle-horn and started up the hill on foot, Paddy crowding close behind. There was no trace of path anywhere and Jed had to pick his steps with care along deep dry gulches channelled by the rush of water in springtime, over glacial deposits of shale and boulder, past dwarfed poplars and evergreen. There were flowers blooming on these upper slopes that he had never seen before, but he could not stop to look at them now. In spite of the uncertain footing he went up quickly. The sweat gathered on his forehead and ran down his face in salty trickles, for the sun was hot now and the wind had almost completely died away. But the

Hog's-Back was close at hand; already Jed could distinguish objects on the skyline – a stunted bush, a pile of rocks forming a natural cairn, a single tree as incongruous in its lonely setting as a human figure would have been.

Now that he was almost at the top Jed suddenly and unaccountably wanted to linger. For the second time he sat down and looked back. Below, the scene had spread out and yet diminished. The horizon had moved farther back; now he was high enough to catch a glimpse of distant emerald-green where a river flowed between enormous banks, of towns so remote that it was impossible to conceive of their having actual being. They were mirages that would vanish with the shimmering heat waves that now hung above the level of the plain. Objects which half an hour ago had seemed close at hand – Joe Palamiro's shack and the Peterson windmill and the upright slab of granite at the mouth the valley called, for no reason anyone knew of, the Dead Man's Needle – had somehow contracted, and slipped away as if carried on the surface of an outgoing tide. Jed sat for a long time until Paddy, dissatisfied with scanty pickings, came close and nuzzled his shoulder.

"All right, all right," Jed said. "We'll be moving."

He mounted and rode on. The ground was bare and brownish grey. Not even the drenching rain of the day previous could restore life to the few wisps of dry grass that lingered near the top, or the tall reedy stems of upland fox-gloves that rattled mournfully in the wind again blowing across the foothills. His father was right, the boy thought, there was no feed up here for a horse. A horse like the Judson grey, he said to himself, in unthinking qualification.

And when he reached the very top at last and was able to look down the opposite side – down a slope that was strange and steep and menacing although he had seen it once before and it had not seemed menacing then – he remembered what his father had said about the

inaccessibility of the Hog's-Back from the Judson side. Dermot was right. No horse could climb that slope. No horse would want to. Jed felt no regret but instead an unexpected lightness of spirit, a strange confusion of happiness and something that made him a little bit afraid. For he had seen a horse on the Hog's-Back – a horse more white than grey. He laughed out loud, then looked quickly at the sun. It was swinging low toward the mountains. It would be twilight in an hour and the dark would come soon afterwards.

He rode along the Hog's-Back until checked by the precipitous side of a dry gully, then returned to the highest point of the arching hill-top, and again looked down the great slope that fell away to the west. The world that way looked different, hill rising above hill until at last they broke into the scintillating splendour of white peaks against a pale blue sky. For no reason at all Jed wanted to cry. Instead he shouted loudly at Paddy and drove his heels into the pony's fat sides.

Paddy trotted a few steps and slowed to a walk. It was then that Jed saw the trees. They were directly below him, just over the first big curve of the west slope. At first he could see only their tops, but as he went down they came completely into view – stunted Balm-of-Gileads that looked curiously unreal in their symmetrical grouping on the barren hillside. And low down, between two grey-green trunks, Jed could see a patch of white.

He rode forward at a walk. Paddy snorted once and Jed pulled hard on the reins. He wanted to turn and ride back up the slope and over the summit towards home. But instead he went on slowly, and the dead weight that dragged at his heart made him faint and sick. He reached the circle of trees. Paddy could smell the water now, although the wind was blowing the other way, and snorted again. But Jed said "no" very quietly and with a funny quaver in his voice. He could see the white patch clearly now, above the surface of the water and partly on the

ground. And he could hear the heavy buzzing noise made
by the swollen blue-bottles as they rose in clouds from the
carcass of the grey horse that had died – quickly or slowly,
it did not matter now – in the treacherous sucking mud
surrounding the hillside spring.

Paddy, scenting death, pawed the ground and whinnied.
Jed swung the pony hard and slapped him with the ends of
the reins. "Giddap-giddap!" he shouted. He rode over the
Hog's-Back at a gallop and on down the other side. Paddy
stumbled and almost fell. Jed pulled him in with a savage
jerk.

"All right, you old geezer," he said. "Take it easy. No
need to break your neck."

It was almost dark when Jed reached home. His father
and mother were in the yard waiting for him. "I was on the
point of starting after you," Dermot shouted, "when we
saw you up there like a god against the setting sun." And
he laughed a great booming laugh that echoed across the
valley.

His mother kissed him on the cheek. "Your father will
put Paddy away, Jed," she said. "I've kept your supper hot
for you."

Jed washed very carefully and combed his hair. He had to comb it several times before he got the parting right. His mother lit the oil-lamp and set it on the table.

"You must be starved, Jed," she said. "I've got a lovely supper for you. Bacon and eggs and the strawberries you picked the day before yesterday."

Dermot came stamping into the kitchen. "And did you lay eyes on the white mustang, son?"

For a minute Jed did not answer. "He's dead," he said at last.

"Dead?"

"It was Judson's grey. He got bogged in a spring."

Astonishment showed in Dermot's face. "So you did see him day before yesterday! But how ever did he get up?"

"There's a stream running down from the spring. He must have followed it up. The grass would be good along the banks."

Dermot filled his pipe. "Too bad, son," he said.

He lit his pipe and blew such clouds of smoke that for a minute his face was almost hidden. "I figure, Jed," he said, somehow talking like one man to another, "that tomorrow you and I had better take a little trip to town."

Jed looked at his father quickly. Dermot blew another cloud of smoke. "The gophers are getting pretty bad. Doesn't seem like we'll be able to keep them down at all unless you get a twenty-two. There's one in Heath's Hardware – nice little single-shot – for seven dollars. I figure we can maybe swing it."

"Gee, Dad," Jed said, "that'll be great."

Suddenly he pushed away his plate. "Mom," he said, "I'm not hungry."

His mother laid her hand on his shoulder. "Would you like to go to bed?" she said.

Jed got up and turned away so that his father could not see his face. He nodded jerkily. His mother spoke to Dermot.

"He's tired out. He'll be all right in the morning."

They went out to the little porch where Jed slept in the summertime. The night air was warm and still and full of rich scents that you didn't notice in daytime. The moon had risen and a band of silver lay across the top of the valley wall opposite. Jed began to cry, silently. His mother put her arms around him without speaking and held him tight.

The door opened and Dermot came out to the porch. "Look at him, would you?" he said, and there was a petulant note in his voice. "All this fuss about a dead horse."

Jed's mother looked at Dermot. When she spoke he could hardly hear her. "Not just a horse, Dermot," she said. "Not an ordinary horse anyway."

And she repeated, matter-of-factly, "He's tired out. He'll be all right in the morning."

Dermot stared at her for a long minute in silence. Then he nodded soberly. "Sure, Mother," he said. "He'll be all right in the morning."

And he closed the door so quietly behind him that it made no noise at all.

GOLDEN THE BEAUTIFUL

ELYNE MITCHELL

from **The Silver Brumby**

Thowra is a silver brumby living in the Australian bush. A fine, wild stallion, he has won the herd of Arrow, his great rival, and with so much to protect he must be more on his guard than ever against his ultimate enemy – man.

THOWRA DID NOT forget that the men had come early last spring, so even when the long fingers of snowdrifts still stretched down the southern slopes and deep snow lay in the gullies, he kept a careful lookout.

He was both proud and embarrassed by the size of his herd now. Besides a rather handsome black mare of Arrow's that he had added to his greys, there were two strange-looking little dun-coloured foals, Arrow's chestnut daughter, and one creamy colt. He did not take much notice of the foals, but he realized that they made his herd slower and less easy to hide.

For a week or more they had been grazing near the headwaters of the Crackenback and Groggin Gap, when one evening, quite late, Thowra heard sounds in the bush, first the jangle of a bit, and then the frou-frou-frou rub of packs on tree-trunks.

He and his herd were not on the stock track, so, telling his mares to stay still, he slipped silently through the already darkening bush, closer and closer to the sounds. Then suddenly he stood absolutely still. Walking along the track, her rider leading one pack-horse, was a cream filly. There were other pack-horses and one stock horse and rider at the end of the procession, but Thowra could look at nothing else but the creamy, with her proud carriage and swinging stride, the lovely silk of her mane and tail.

For a while, he moved silently through the trees parallel with the track, watching and watching her.

The men seemed to be tired out and swaying, half-asleep in their saddles. They did not even hear her whinnying softly when she looked through the bush and saw Thowra.

Thowra knew quite well that the men must be going to the Dead Horse hut, their pack-horses loaded with stores of tinned foods, and flour, and salt for the cattle. He turned back to his herd to put them in a safe place for the night, knowing that he must return to the hut himself. A half moon came up a few hours later, enough to see by and yet not so light that Thowra could not keep himself well hidden.

Before going very near the hut, he walked along the horse-paddock fence. He could see the pack-horses, moving like restless shadows, but there was no sign of the two riding-horses, neither the creamy nor the other whose colour he had not even noticed. He had rather expected that they would be left in that new yard whose high fences he and Storm had studied more than a year ago.

The timber was cleared quite a long way back from the yard, which stood out on its own against the horse-paddock fence, in front of the hut.

Thowra moved through the trees very slowly, seeking the dark pools of shadow and avoiding any glades where the moonlight shone. A possum watched him with its wistful yet curious, pointed face. It gave a deep, throaty qua-a-r-rk, and he heard the sound of horses shuffling in the yard. He stood at the edge of the trees looking across. Yes, there, silvered by moonlight, was the lovely filly. She whinnied softly again, and a man opened the hut door, the light from a hurricane lamp blending with the moonlight.

A voice said, "The brumbies might be about." And another voice inside the hut answered: "Don't worry. The fence is mighty high, but you was a fool to bring her, all the same." Then they shut the door again and soon the hurricane lamp was turned out.

After waiting a long time, Thowra walked across the open ground to the yard. The cream filly came up to the fence, trembling with excitement, and put her nose through to snuff him.

As she started to whinny he said:

"No. No. You must learn to be silent, if you would come with me. What is your name?"

"They call me Golden. You must be Thowra of whom all the other horses speak – and the men even have songs about you that they sing to the cattle, but they call you Silver."

"Thowra is my name," said Thowra proudly. "The name my mother, Bel Bel, gave me."

Just then the bay stock horse, who had been standing trembling in the yard, let out a shrill, ringing neigh. Thowra was gone in a flash, silent-footed but fast, back into the bush. He was barely hidden in the trees before he heard the hut door opening and saw a man come out with a torch. Thowra watched him go right over to the yard, where the horse and the cream filly stood snorting, and turn his torch on to the ground. When he heard him say, "Huh, an unshod horse!" Thowra knew it was time to go, and to go on rocks and grass where he left no track.

Last year the men who had brought the pack-horses out early had stayed two nights. These men would probably too – but would they perhaps hobble the horses the next night, or watch over them in turns, hoping to catch him? He decided to wait till later in the night and then go back.

The moon had gone behind a bank of cloud when Thowra next stood on the edge of the bush and peered through the leathery snowgum leaves towards the yard. He could see Golden moving restlessly about, but the other horse seemed to be asleep.

Stepping from one snowgrass tussock to another, he moved towards the yard again, this time making for the only place in the fence where there was grass and not bare earth.

Golden came up to him again.

"How high can you jump?" Thowra asked her. "There is one lower place in this fence over there in the corner."

"I'd never clear that," said Golden.

28

"Not even if I jumped in and gave you a lead out over it?" But he eyed the bay horse. With that silly jackass there to bray, the game would be given away before they could get out.

Just then the bay horse stirred; he threw up his head with a startled snort, and then neighed loudly.

"Jump, and come with me," Thowra said, as he turned to go. Already there was a clatter in the hut and a man's voice cursing.

Thowra bounded away over the grass. He looked back, but Golden was not following, and before he had quite reached the trees he heard the door open. He was hidden by the time the man appeared but it had been a near thing. Thowra watched the man prowling around, saw that he could find no more tracks and that he was puzzled. Presently he went back inside, but there were still sounds of him moving about, and then came the smell of smoke as it poured through the hut chimney.

Just then the dawn wind came, stirring the darkness of the night, touching with cool, long fingers Thowra's coat, his ears; whispering through the snowgum leaves. Daylight would soon come, and he must not be seen, but he could not tear himself away and he remained, never taking his eyes off the yard. The man came out with a pannikin of tea in his hand and leant on the yard fence. He called Golden. To Thowra's amazement he saw her walk over to him and take something out of his hand and eat it.

Thowra tossed his head and turned away into the thick bush. He made no sound as he went back to his herd, but Golden's whinny followed him. He stopped for a second and listened, not understanding how she could whinny to him and yet accept something from the man. But the whinny sealed his determination to get her for himself.

The presence of his own herd made it awkward. He realized that fully when he came through the trees and found them in a glade that was filled with the liquid gold of early morning sunshine. They looked beautiful, his greys with their tiny odd-coloured foals, and the one lovely cream one. He must not take the chance of being chased by the men himself, and his herd being found – but how wonderful it would be to have Golden there with the greys.

That morning he led the herd up towards the Ramshead, and put them in a gully that opened to the north-west and was bare of snow. Then he turned back to the hut, going carefully and quietly through the thickest bush, and leaving hardly a hoofmark.

All his senses were alert. He heard the faintest rustle made by an early-moving snake, saw its beady eye. He felt, before he saw, the gang-gangs looking at him, their red crests up. When two kangaroos went hopping by rather quickly he went more carefully still. Then, in the distance, he heard the sound of a shod horse. Thowra slid farther into the thick scrub, and stood waiting.

Presently he heard two horses approaching, and when he knew they had passed, he drew closer. There were the two men riding Golden and the bay horse. The packs must have been left behind, which meant the men would stay another night. He followed for a while to see what they were doing.

They were wandering without direction, looking for something – and, if it were his tracks they were looking for, they were wasting their time, because they were not going to find any.

He turned back to the hut and had a look around. The pack-horses were grazing in the horse paddock. Everything was as he thought. He headed for the Ramshead and the herd.

That night Thowra went to the hut again, stepping proudly through the dark forest before the moon had risen. Leaves brushed his shoulder and there was a lovely damp scent of the bush at night. He kept thinking of what Bel Bel would say to such a foolhardy expedition as this – and yet he knew she would understand. She was creamy herself and could appreciate how lovely the cream filly was. It was Storm who would really consider him a fool.

He kept watch for a long time from the edge of the trees, slightly surprised that Golden showed no sign of knowing he was there, but he had been even more silent than before, and Golden's senses were not as sharp as a wild horse's.

The fire and the lamp were both out in the hut, and all was quiet. He could see no man watching over the horses, and the horses were not hobbled. Still suspecting a trap, he came out of the trees slowly, thankful that the moon had not yet risen. He reached the fence, his skin pricking with nervousness, but nothing happened. The bay was sound asleep.

He measured up the fence again, and in the springtime surge of strength and spirits, he felt sure that he would be able to jump out and lead Golden away.

He backed off, speeded up as quietly as he could, and jumped.

"Now, come on and follow me!" he said to Golden.

The bay woke with a startled squeal. A man burst out of the hut, shouting:

"Got you, my beauty!"

31

"Come quick!" said Thowra, and with only the very short run available in the yard, he took three strides and made a prodigious leap. His knees rapped the top rail, yet he still seemed to lift higher. A rope whistled and fell short. Thowra felt his heart almost bursting with fear and effort, but he was over! The other man was running with a rope, too.

Thowra swung wildly and felt it hit his flank. Golden called, but she was still in the yard. The first man had roped her, but Thowra did not know this. He called in answer, but she still did not come. He galloped towards the trees, hearing the men getting saddles and bridles. But a brumby stallion who knew the country would get a good start while they saddled up. He raced away towards the Cascades, taking the opposite direction to that in which his herd lay, the one the men might easily expect him to take.

Through the night he galloped, darkness like a curtain around him. A white owl flew, crying, from a tree and he shied in sudden fear. He could hear the men close behind, so he branched off the track and down a rock gully; the men, when they found they could not easily capture him, soon gave up. The owner of Golden had no wish to lame her in a midnight brumby hunt, and anyway it was obvious that Golden might very well bait a trap for Thowra. They decided to stay at the hut another night.

In the morning they built up the rails on the lowest side of the yard.

Thowra watched the track to Groggin and knew that they had not gone down from the mountains; he watched the sky, too, because he could see that bad weather was coming, and sensed that it was coming very quickly. When the men had not gone by mid-afternoon, he hastened off to his herd and took them lower down the Crackenback, where, if there were snow, they would be sheltered. Before they had reached the glade to which he was taking them, the wind was howling over the mountain-top and bringing with it biting flakes of snow. The foals were frightened and kept getting under their mothers' feet. Thowra felt responsible for them and stayed with them in the gathering storm. His knees were bruised and stiff from their rap on the fence, and he was glad to be with his mares.

All night long the cold snow fell. At Dead Horse hut the men gave up hoping for the cream stallion to come, and worried about their own horses. The pack-horses were better off than the two riding-horses because there were trees in the paddock under which they could shelter.

Golden's owner was particularly worried. There was not room for even one horse to stand in the skillion; it was full of wood and bags of salt.

At midnight they decided to turn them out of the yard into the horse paddock. Already the snow lay inches deep on the ground; covered rails and fence-posts; slithered with a soft thud off the trees. The cream filly and the bay horse walked gladly through the gate and towards a clump of trees.

The men sloshed their way through the snow back to the hut, shook the flakes off their coats, threw more wood on the fire, and settled down again for what remained of the night.

It was in the heavy, dark hours of the very early morning, when the blizzard was at its height, that Thowra came.

He had to walk right to the yard before he was sure it was empty, then he went, silent-footed in the snow, right up to the skillion, but there was nothing there. He went back to the horse-paddock fence and followed it till it went through some trees. Here he could hear the snuffling and shuffling of quite a number of horses and guessed Golden would be with them.

He retreated a little way until he found a panel of fencing over which he thought he might be able to jump – it was not so much the height of the fence that bothered him, but rather where it was and where to jump – in the blizzard it was difficult to see anything clearly. He cantered towards it, making an enormous leap.

The snow beat in his eyes, hit his legs, his chest, his belly. He was flying through the blizzard – waiting for the ghastly check of biting barbed wire if he had miscalculated his jump. But there was no check, no terrible bite of wire on his legs. He slithered a little on landing and drew a huge breath of relief. He was safely over!

34

He jogged down the fence line until he came to the trees, then sneaked in, moving silently from tree to tree, conscious of every sound, feeling the cold touch of the snow on his coat. It was easy to see the dark-coloured horses, as he drew close to them, but Golden, like himself, was invisible in the snowstorm, and it was Golden he must find.

He had circled right round the group of horses before he found her, standing on her own under a tree by the fence. Straining his eyes, he could just see her outline, sensed that she had become suddenly tense, and he knew then that she had seen him. She stood quite still.

"Will you follow me, now?" he asked. "I will jump the fence and stand beside it so that you can see where it is. This fence is not too high for you to jump."

He could tell she was trembling with nervousness, but he did not understand that she was torn between her desire to go with him and her instinct to stay obediently where she was.

He moved off and she followed, back to the panel in the fence which he had jumped before. He took her to the fence and told her to make certain she knew how high she must leap.

The snow was driving behind Thowra this time; the wind almost lifted him, and he was so excited that he felt no fear of jumping too early or too late, or not high enough. When he landed he turned back and stood by the fences neighing softly. For a moment he thought that Golden would not come; then she came, invisible – though he could hear her galloping – till she was right at the fence and taking off in a wildly high jump. She, too, was over and free.

THE FIREBIRD, THE HORSE OF POWER AND THE PRINCESS VASILISSA

ARTHUR RANSOME

ONCE UPON A TIME a strong and powerful Tzar ruled in a country far away. And among his servants was a young archer, and this archer had a horse – a horse of power – such a horse as belonged to the wonderful men of long ago – a great horse with a broad chest, eyes like fire, and hoofs of iron. There are no such horses nowadays. They sleep with the strong men who rode them, the bogatirs, until the time comes when Russia has need of them. Then the great horses will thunder up from under the ground, and the valiant men leap from the graves in the armour they have worn so long. The strong men will sit those horses of power, and there will be swinging of clubs and thunder of hoofs, and the earth will be swept clean from the enemies of God and the Tzar. So my grandfather used to say, and he was as much older than I as I am older than you, little ones, and so he should know.

Well, one day long ago, in the green time of the year, the young archer rode through the forest on his horse of power. The trees were green; there were little blue flowers on the ground under the trees; the squirrels ran in the branches, and the hares in the undergrowth; but no birds sang. The young archer rode along the forest path and listened for the singing of the birds, but there was no singing. The forest was silent, and the only noises in it were the scratching of four-footed beasts, the dropping of fir cones, and the heavy stamping of the horse of power in the soft path.

"What has come to the birds?" said the young archer.

He had scarcely said this before he saw a big curving feather lying in the path before him. The feather was larger than a swan's, larger than an eagle's. It lay in the path, glittering like a flame; for the sun was on it, and it was a feather of pure gold. Then he knew why there was no singing in the forest. For he knew that the firebird had flown that way, and that the feather in the path before him was a feather from its burning breast.

The horse of power spoke and said:

"Leave the golden feather where it lies. If you take it you will be sorry for it, and know the meaning of fear."

But the brave young archer sat on the horse of power and looked at the golden feather, and wondered whether to take it or not. He had no wish to learn what it was to be afraid, but he thought, "If I take it and bring it to the Tzar my master, he will be pleased; and he will not send me away with empty hands, for no tzar in the world has a feather from the burning breast of the firebird." And the more he thought, the more he wanted to carry the feather to the Tzar. And in the end he did not listen to the words of the horse of power. He leaped from the saddle, picked up the golden feather of the firebird, mounted his horse again, and galloped back through the green forest till he came to the palace of the Tzar.

He went into the palace, and bowed before the Tzar and said:

"O Tzar, I have brought you a feather of the firebird."

The Tzar looked gladly at the feather, and then at the young archer.

"Thank you," says he; "but if you have brought me a feather of the firebird, you will be able to bring me the bird itself. I should like to see it. A feather is not a fit gift to bring to the Tzar. Bring the bird itself, or, I swear by my sword, your head shall no longer sit between your shoulders!"

The younger archer bowed his head and went out. Bitterly he wept, for he knew what it was to be afraid. He went out into the courtyard, where the horse of power was waiting for him, tossing his head and stamping on the ground.

"Master," says the horse of power, "why do you weep?"

"The Tzar has told me to bring him the firebird, and no man on earth can do that," says the young archer, and he bowed his head on his breast.

"I told you," says the horse of power, "that if you took the feather you would learn the meaning of fear. Well, do not be frightened yet, and do not weep. The trouble is not now; the trouble lies before you. Go to the Tzar and ask him to have a hundred sacks of maize scattered over the open field, and let this be done at midnight."

The young archer went back into the palace and begged the Tzar for this, and the Tzar ordered that at midnight a hundred sacks of maize should be scattered in the open field.

Next morning, at the first redness in the sky, the young archer rode out on the horse of power, and came to the open field. The ground was scattered all over with maize. In the middle of the field stood a great oak with spreading boughs. The young archer leaped to the ground, took off the saddle, and let the horse of power loose to wander as he pleased about the field. Then he climbed up into the oak and hid himself among the green boughs.

The sky grew red and gold, and the sun rose. Suddenly there was a noise in the forest round the field. The trees shook and swayed, and almost fell. There was a mighty wind. The sea piled itself into waves with crests of foam, and the firebird came flying from the other side of the world. Huge and golden and flaming in the sun, it flew, dropped down with open wings into the field, and began to eat the maize.

The horse of power wandered in the field. This way he went, and that, but always he came a little nearer to the firebird. Nearer and nearer came the horse. He came close up to the firebird, and then suddenly stepped on one of its spreading fiery wings and pressed it heavily to the ground. The bird struggled, flapping mightily with its fiery wings, but it could not get away. The young archer slipped down from the tree, bound the firebird with three strong ropes, swung it on his back, saddled the horse, and rode to the palace of the Tzar.

The young archer stood before the Tzar, and his back

was bent under the great weight of the firebird, and the broad wings of the bird hung on either side of him like fiery shields, and there was a trail of golden feathers on the floor. The young archer swung the magic bird to the foot of the throne before the Tzar; and the Tzar was glad, because since the beginning of the world no tzar had seen the firebird flung before him like a wild duck caught in a snare.

The Tzar looked at the firebird and laughed with pride. Then he lifted his eyes and looked at the young archer, and says he:

"As you have known how to take the firebird, you will know how to bring me my bride, for whom I have long been waiting. In the land of Never, on the very edge of the world, where the red sun rises in flame from behind the sea, lives the Princess Vasilissa. I will marry none but her. Bring her to me, and I will reward you with silver and gold. But if you do not bring her, then, by my sword, your head will no longer sit between your shoulders!"

The young archer wept bitter tears, and went out into the courtyard where the horse of power was stamping the ground with its hoofs of iron and tossing its thick mane.

"Master, why do you weep?" asked the horse of power.

"The Tzar has ordered me to go to the land of Never, and to bring back the Princess Vasilissa."

"Do not weep – do not grieve. The trouble is not yet; the trouble is to come. Go to the Tzar and ask him for a silver tent with a golden roof, and for all kinds of food and drink to take with us on the journey."

The young archer went in and asked the Tzar for this, and the Tzar gave him a silver tent with silver hangings and a gold-embroidered roof, and every kind of rich wine and the tastiest of foods.

Then the young archer mounted the horse of power and rode off to the land of Never. On and on he rode, many days and nights, and came at last to the edge of the world, where the red sun rises in flame from behind the deep blue sea.

On the shore of the sea the young archer reined in the horse of power, and the heavy hoofs of the horse sank in the sand. He shaded his eyes and looked out over the blue water, and there was the Princess Vasilissa in a little silver boat, rowing with golden oars.

The young archer rode back a little way to where the sand ended and the green world began. There he loosed the horse to wander where he pleased, and to feed on the green grass. Then on the edge of the shore, where the green grass ended and grew thin and the sand began, he set up the shining tent, with its silver hangings and its gold-embroidered roof. In the tent he set out the tasty dishes and the rich flagons of wine which the Tzar had given him, and he sat himself down in the tent and began to regale himself, while he waited for the Princess Vasilissa.

The Princess Vasilissa dipped her golden oars in the blue water, and the little silver boat moved lightly through the dancing waves. She sat in the little boat and looked over the blue sea to the edge of the world, and there, between the golden sand and the green earth, she saw the tent standing, silver and gold in the sun. She dipped her oars, and came nearer to see·it better. The nearer she came the fairer seemed the tent, and at˙last she rowed to the shore and grounded her little boat on the golden sand, and stepped out daintily and came up to the tent. She was a little frightened, and now and again she stopped and looked back to where the silver boat lay on the sand with the blue sea beyond it. The young archer said not a word, but went on regaling himself on the pleasant dishes he had set out there in the tent.

At last the Princess Vasilissa came up to the tent and looked in.

The young archer rose and bowed before her. Says he:

"Good day to you, Princess! Be so kind as to come in and take bread and salt with me, and taste my foreign wines."

And the Princess Vasilissa came into the tent and sat down with the young archer, and ate sweetmeats with him, and drank his health in a golden goblet of the wine the Tzar had given him. Now this wine was heavy, and the last drop from the goblet had no sooner trickled down her little slender throat than her eyes closed against her will, once, twice, and again.

"Ah me!" says the Princess, "it is as if the night itself had perched on my eyelids, and yet it is but noon."

And the golden goblet dropped to the ground from her little fingers, and she leaned back on a cushion and fell instantly asleep. If she had been beautiful before, she was lovelier when she lay in that deep sleep in the shadow of the tent.

Quickly the young archer called to the horse of power. Lightly he lifted the Princess in his strong young arms. Swiftly he leaped with her into the saddle. Like a feather

she lay in the hollow of his left arm, and slept while the iron hoofs of the great horse thundered over the ground.

They came to the Tzar's palace, and the young archer leaped from the horse of power and carried the Princess into the palace. Great was the joy of the Tzar; but it did not last for long.

"Go, sound the trumpets for our wedding," he said to his servants, "let all the bells be rung."

The bells rang out and the trumpets sounded, and at the noise of the horns and the ringing of the bells the Princess Vasilissa woke up and looked about her.

"What is this ringing of bells," says she, "and this noise of trumpets? And where, oh, where is the blue sea, and my little silver boat with its golden oars?" And the Princess put her hand to her eyes.

"The blue sea is far away," says the Tzar, "and for your little silver boat I give you a golden throne. The trumpets sound for our wedding, and the bells are ringing for our joy."

But the Princess turned her face away from the Tzar; and there was no wonder in that, for he was old, and his eyes were not kind.

And she looked with love at the young archer; and there

was no wonder in that either, for he was a young man fit to ride the horse of power.

The Tzar was angry with the Princess Vasilissa, but his anger was as useless as his joy.

"Why, Princess," says he, "will you not marry me, and forget your blue sea and your silver boat?"

"In the middle of the deep blue sea lies a great stone," says the Princess, "and under that stone is hidden my wedding dress. If I cannot wear that dress I will marry nobody at all."

Instantly the Tzar turned to the young archer, who was waiting before the throne.

"Ride swiftly back," says he, "to the land of Never, where the red sun rises in flame. There – do you hear what the Princess says? – a great stone lies in the middle of the sea. Under that stone is hidden her wedding dress. Ride swiftly. Bring back that dress, or, by my sword, your head shall no longer sit between your shoulders!"

The young archer wept bitter tears, and went out into the courtyard, where the horse of power was waiting for him, champing its golden bit.

"There is no way of escaping death this time," he said.

"Master, why do you weep?" asked the horse of power.

"The Tzar has ordered me to ride to the land of Never, to fetch the wedding dress of the Princess Vasilissa from the bottom of the deep blue sea. Besides, the dress is wanted for the Tzar's wedding, and I love the Princess myself."

"What did I tell you?" says the horse of power. "I told you that there would be trouble if you picked up the golden feather from the firebird's burning breast. Well, do not be afraid. The trouble is not yet; the trouble is to come. Up! into the saddle with you, and away for the wedding dress of the Princess Vasilissa!"

The young archer leaped into the saddle, and the horse of power, with his thundering hoofs, carried him swiftly through the green forests and over the bare plains, till they came to the edge of the world, to the land of Never, where the red sun rises in flame from behind the deep blue sea. There they rested, at the very edge of the sea.

The young archer looked sadly over the wide waters, but the horse of power tossed its mane and did not look at the sea, but on the shore. This way and that it looked, and saw at last a huge lobster moving slowly, sideways, along the golden sand.

Nearer and nearer came the lobster, and it was a giant among lobsters, the tzar of all the lobsters; and it moved slowly along the shore, while the horse of power moved carefully and as if by accident, until it stood between the lobster and the sea. Then when the lobster came close by, the horse of power lifted an iron hoof and set it firmly on the lobster's tail.

"You will be death of me!" screamed the lobster – as well he might, with the heavy foot of the horse of power pressing his tail into the sand. "Let me live, and I will do whatever you ask of me."

"Very well," says the horse of power, "we will let you live," and he slowly lifted his foot. "But this is what you shall do for us. In the middle of the blue sea lies a great stone, and under that stone is hidden the wedding dress of the Princess Vasilissa. Bring it here."

The lobster groaned with the pain in his tail. Then he cried out in a voice that could be heard all over the deep blue sea. And the sea was disturbed, and from all sides lobsters in thousands made their way toward the bank. And the huge lobster that was the oldest of them all and the tzar of all the lobsters that live between the rising and the setting of the sun, gave them the order and sent them back into the sea. And the young archer sat on the horse of power and waited.

After a little time the sea was disturbed again, and the lobsters in their thousands came to the shore, and with them they brought a golden casket in which was the wedding dress of the Princess Vasilissa. They had taken it from under the great stone that lay in the middle of the sea.

The tzar of all the lobsters raised himself painfully on his bruised tail and gave the casket into the hands of the young archer, and instantly the horse of power turned himself about and galloped back to the palace of the Tzar, far, far away, at the other side of the green forests and beyond the treeless plains.

The young archer went into the palace and gave the casket into the hands of the Princess, and looked at her with sadness in his eyes and she looked at him with love. Then she went away into an inner chamber, and came back in her wedding dress, fairer than spring itself. Great was the joy of the Tzar. The wedding feast was made ready, and the bells rang, and flags waved about the palace.

The Tzar held out his hand to the Princess, and looked at her with his old eyes. But she would not take his hand.

"No," says she, "I will marry nobody until the man who brought me here has done penance in boiling water."

Instantly the Tzar turned to his servants and ordered them to make a great fire, and to fill a great cauldron with water and set it on the fire, and, when the water should be at its hottest, to take the young archer and throw him into it, to do penance for having taken the Princess Vasilissa away from the land of Never.

There was no gratitude in the mind of that Tzar.

Swiftly the servants brought wood and made a mighty fire, and on it they laid a huge cauldron of water, and built the fire round the walls of the cauldron. The fire burned hot and the water steamed. The fire burned hotter, and the water bubbled and seethed. They made ready to take the young archer, to throw him into the cauldron.

"Oh, misery!" thought the young archer. "Why did I ever take the golden feather that had fallen from the firebird's burning breast? Why did I not listen to the wise words of the horse of power?" And he remembered the horse of power, and he begged the Tzar:

"O lord Tzar, I do not complain. I shall presently die in the heat of the water on the fire. Suffer me, before I die, once more to see my horse."

"Let him see his horse," says the Princess.

"Very well," says the Tzar. "Say good-bye to your horse, for you will not ride him again. But let your farewells be short, for we are waiting."

The young archer crossed the courtyard and came to the horse of power, who was scraping the ground with his iron hoofs.

"Farewell, my horse of power," says the young archer. "I should have listened to your words of wisdom, for now the end is come, and we shall never more see the green trees pass above us and the ground disappear beneath us, as we race the wind between the earth and the sky."

"Why so?" says the horse of power.

"The Tzar has ordered that I am to be boiled to death –

thrown into that cauldron that is seething on the great fire."

"Fear not," says the horse of power, "for the Princess Vasilissa has made him do this, and the end of these things is better than I thought. Go back, and when they are ready to throw you in the cauldron, do you run boldly and leap yourself into the boiling water."

The young archer went back across the courtyard, and the servants made ready to throw him into the cauldron.

"Are you sure that the water is boiling?" says the Princess Vasilissa.

"It bubbles and seethes," said the servants.

"Let me see for myself," says the Princess, and she went to the fire and waved her hand above the cauldron. And some say there was something in her hand, and some say there was not.

"It is boiling," says she, and the servants laid hands on the young archer; but he threw them from him, and ran and leaped boldly before them all into the very middle of the cauldron.

Twice he sank below the surface, borne round with the bubbles and foam of the boiling water. Then he leaped from the cauldron and stood before the Tzar and the Princess. He had become so beautiful a youth that all who saw cried aloud in wonder.

"This is a miracle," says the Tzar. And the Tzar looked at the beautiful young archer, and thought of himself – of his age, of his bent back, and his grey beard, and his toothless gums. "I too will become beautiful," thinks he, and he rose from his throne and clambered into the cauldron, and was boiled to death in a moment.

And the end of the story? They buried the Tzar, and made the young archer Tzar in his place. He married the Princess Vasilissa, and lived many years with her in love and good fellowship. And he built a golden stable for the horse of power, and never forgot what he owed to him.

NATIONAL VELVET

ENID BAGNOLD

Velvet is fulfilling her greatest dream and riding in the Grand National on her horse, The Piebald. Because race rules don't allow female jockeys, she is disguised as a boy. Mi, the horse's trainer, rushes through the crowds so he can see Velvet ride in this most famous, and dangerous, of races.

AT THE POST the twenty horses were swaying like the sea. Forward . . . No Good! Back again. Forward . . . No good! Back again.

The line formed . . . and rebroke. Waves of the sea. Drawing a breath . . . breaking. Velvet fifth from the rail, between a bay and a brown. The Starter had long finished his instructions. Nothing more was said aloud, but low oaths flew, the cursing and grumbling flashed like a storm. An eye glanced at her with a look of hate. The breaking of movement was too close to movement to be borne. It was like water clinging to the tilted rim of the glass, like the sound of the dreaded explosion after the great shell has fallen. The will to surge forward overlaid by something delicate and terrible and strong, human obedience at bursting-point, but not broken. Horses' eyes gleamed openly, men's eyes set like chips of steel. Rough man,

50

checked in violence, barely master of himself, barely master of his horse. The Piebald ominously quiet, and nothing coming from him . . . up went the tape.

The green Course poured in a river before her as she lay forward, and with the plunge of movement sat in the stream.

"Black slugs . . ." said Mi, cursing under his breath, running, dodging, suffocated with the crowd. It was the one thing he had overlooked, that the crowd was too dense to allow him to reach Becher's in the time. Away up above him was the truckline, his once-glorious free seat, separated from him by a fence. "God's liver," he mumbled, his throat gone cold, and stumbled into an old fool in a mackintosh. "Are they off?" he yelled at the heavy crowd as he ran, but no one bothered with him.

He was cursed if he was heeded at all. He ran, gauging his position by the cranes on the embankment. Velvet coming over Becher's in a minute and he not there to see her. "They're off!" All around him a sea of throats offered up the gasp.

He was opposite Becher's but could see nothing: the crowd thirty deep between him and the Course. All around fell the terrible silence of expectancy. Mi stood like a rock. If he could not see then he must use his ears, hear. Enclosed in the dense, silent, dripping pack he heard the thunder coming. It roared up on the wet turf like the single approach of a multiple-footed animal. There were stifled exclamations, grunts, thuds. Something in the air flashed and descended. The first over Becher's! A roar went up from the crowd, then silence. The things flashing in the air were indistinguishable. The tip of a cap exposed for the briefest of seconds. The race went by like an express train, and was gone. Could Velvet be alive in that?

Sweat ran off Mi's forehead and into his eyes. But it was not sweat that turned the air grey and blotted out the faces before him. The ground on all sides seemed to be smoking.

An extraordinary mist, like a low prairie fire, was formed in the air. It had dwelt heavily all day behind the Canal, but the whole of the Course had remained clear till now. And now, before you could turn to look at your neighbour, his face was gone. The mist blew in shreds, drifted, left the crowd clear again but hid the whole of the Canal Corner, fences, stand and horses.

There was a struggle going on at Becher's; a horse had fallen and was being got out with ropes. Mi's legs turned to water and he asked his neighbour gruffly,

"Who's fallen?" But the neighbour, straining to the tip of his toes, and glued to his glasses, was deaf as lead.

Suddenly Mi lashed round him in a frenzy. "Who's fallen, I say? Who's hurt?"

"Steady on," said a little man whom he had prodded in the stomach.

"Who's fallen?" said Mi desperately. "I gotta brother in this . . ."

"It's his brother!" said the crowd all around him. "Let him through."

Mi was pushed and pummelled to the front and remained embedded two from the front line. The horse that had fallen was a black horse, its neck unnaturally stretched by the ropes that were hauling it from the ditch.

There was a shout and a horse, not riderless, but ridden by a tugging, cursing man, came galloping back through the curling fumes of the mist, rolled its wild eye at the wrong side of Becher's and disappeared away out of the Course. An uproar began along the fringes of the crowd and rolled back to where Mi stood. Two more horses came back out of the mist, one riderless. The shades of others could be discerned in the fog. Curses rapped out from the unseen mouths.

"What's happened at the Canal Turn? What's wrong down at the Turn?"

"The whole field!" shouted a man. The crowd took it up.

"The field's out. The whole field's come back. There's no

race!" It was unearthly. Something a hundred yards down there in the fog had risen up and destroyed the greatest steeplechase in the world.

Nineteen horses had streamed down to the Canal Turn, and suddenly, there across the Course, at the boundary of the fog, four horses appeared beyond Valentine's, and among them, fourth, was The Piebald.

"Yer little lovely, yer little lovely!" yelled Mi, wringing his hands and hitting his knees. "It's her, it's him, it's me brother!"

No one took any notice. The scene immediately before them occupied all the attention. Horses that had fallen galloped by riderless, stirrups flying from their saddles, jockeys returned on foot, covered with mud, limping, holding their sides, some running slowly and miserably over the soggy course, trying to catch and sort the horses.

"It's 'Yellow Messenger'," said a jockey savagely, who had just seized his horse. "Stuck on the fence down there and kicking hell." And he mounted.

"And wouldn't they jump over him?" called a girl shrilly.

"They didn't wanter hurt the poor thing, lady," said the jockey, grinning through his mud, and rode off.

"Whole lot piled up and refused," said a man who came up the line. "Get the Course clear now, quick!"

"They're coming again!" yelled Mi, watching the galloping four. "Get the Course clear! They'll be coming!'

They were out of his vision now, stuck down under Becher's high fence as he was. Once past Becher's on the second round would he have time to extricate himself and get back to the post before they were home? He stood indecisively and a minute went by. The Course in front of him was clear. Horses and men had melted. The hush of anticipation began to fall. "They're on the tan again," said a single voice. Mi flashed to a decision. He could not afford the minutes to be at Becher's. He must get back for the finish and it would take him all his time. He backed and plunged and ducked, got cursed afresh. The thunder was coming again as he reached the road and turned to face the far-off Stands. This time he could see nothing at all, not even a cap in the air. "What's leading? What's leading?"

"Big Brown. Tantibus, Tantibus. Tantibus leading."

"Where's The Piebald?"

"See that! Leonora coming up . . ."

They were deaf to his frantic questions. He could not wait but ran. The mist was ahead of him again, driving in frills and wafting sedgily about. Could Velvet have survived Becher's twice? In any case no good wondering. He couldn't get at her to help her. If she fell he would find her more quickly at the hospital door. Better that than struggle through the crowd and be forbidden the now empty Course.

Then a yell. "There's one down!"

"It's the Yank mare!"

The horse ambulance was trundling back with Yellow Messenger from the Canal Turn. Mi leapt for a second on to the turning hub of the wheel, and saw in a flash, across the momentarily mist-clear course, the pride of Baltimore in the mud underneath Valentine's. The Piebald was lying third. The wheel turned and he could see no more. Five fences from the finish; he would not allow himself to hope, but ran and ran. How far away the Stands in the gaps of the mist as he pushed, gasping, through the people. Would she fall now? What had he done, bringing her up here? But would she fall now? He ran and ran.

"They're coming on to the Racecourse . . . coming on to the Racecourse . . ."

"How many?"

"Rain, rain, can't see a thing."

"How many?"

Down sank the fog again, as a puff of wind blew and gathered it together. There was a steady roaring from the Stands, then silence, then a hub-bub. No one could see the telegraph.

Mi running, gasped, "Who's won?"

But everyone was asking the same question. Men were running, pushing, running, just as he. He came up to the gates of Melling Road, crossed the road on the fringe of the tan, and suddenly, out of the mist, The Piebald galloped riderless, lolloping unsteadily along, reins hanging, stirrups dangling. Mi burst through on to the Course, his heart wrung.

"Get back there!" shouted a policeman. "Loose horse!"

"Hullo, Old Pie there!" shouted Mi. The animal, soaked, panting, spent, staggered and slipped and drew up.

"What've you done with 'er?" asked Mi, weeping, and bent down to lift the hoof back through the rein. "You let 'er down, Pie? What in God's sake?" He led the horse down the Course, running, his breath catching, his heart thumping, tears and rain on his face.

Two men came towards him out of the mist.

"You got him?" shouted one. "Good fer you. Gimme!"

"You want him?" said Mi, in a stupor, giving up the rein.

"Raised an objection. Want him for the enclosure. Chap come queer."

"Chap did? What chap?"

"This here's the winner! Where you bin all day, Percy?"

"Foggy," said Mi. "Very foggy. Oh my God!"

"Taken him round to the hospital."

"Stretcher, was it?"

"Jus' gone through where all those people are . . ."

The doctor had got back from his tour of the Course in his ambulance. Two riders had already been brought in and the nurse had prepared them in readiness for his examination. Now the winner himself coming in on a stretcher. Busy thirty minutes ahead.

"Could you come here a minute?" said the Sister, at his side a few minutes later.

She whispered to him quietly. He slapped his rain-coated cheek and went to the bed by the door. "Put your screens round." She planted them. "Constable," he said, poking his head out of the door, "get one of the Stewards here, will you." (The roar of the crowd came in at the door.) "One of the Stewards! Quick's you can. Here, I'll let you in this side door. You can get through." The crowd seethed, seizing upon every sign.

Mi crouched by the door without daring to ask after his child. He heard the doctor call. He saw the Steward to go in. "Anyway," he thought, "they've found out at once. They would. What's it matter if she's all right? She's won, the little beggar, the little beggar. Oh my God!"

THE BROKEN BRIDGE

REGINALD OTTLEY

THE RAIN ROARED DOWN – great driving sheets of it, that rattled the corrugated iron.

Hunched over a table in the rough Bush hut, I knew I had to make a decision. If the rain kept on much longer, as well it might, I could be stranded for weeks. Yet if I left immediately, I had no way of knowing how much flood damage had already been done; though I did know I would get a cold, sodden soaking.

At last I said, "Well, it's not gettin' any easier. This is the third day now, an' you'll soon be out of tucker. Besides, I'd better get that mare home."

Bill, the boundary rider whose hut it was, nodded. He was a big quiet man who had offered me shelter when the rain started.

"Yeah," he said. "If that's how you see it. I don't mind the tucker, but the other's up to you."

I agreed that it was, and rolled my blankets. Outside in the teeming rain I strapped them to my saddle. Then I humped the whole – saddle, bridle and blanket roll – over to the horse-yards. In one of them stood Midnight, my saddle-horse. In another, was the brood mare I was leading home from a distant property. She was heavy in foal, and could give birth any time. A previously injured leg, now healed, had stopped her from being taken home sooner.

As I saddled Midnight, he stood staring beyond me to the brood mare. Maybe he sensed something – I don't know. He was a strange horse; bad, some would have called him. I had broken him some weeks before, but he had never accepted the breaking. Oh yes, I could ride and steer him, though never without a fight. Yet of all the horses I have known – and they have been many – I loved him the greatest. There was an indomitable fire in him that could never be extinguished.

Wondering what he had in store for me, I saddled and bridled Midnight while Bill put a halter on Moonlight, the mare. She was a silvery dapple grey, bedraggled now from the pouring rain.

As Bill led her close I swung up on to Midnight. To ride a wild bucking horse on a bright sunny day is one thing. To ride Midnight, prince of all buck-jumpers, in a storming swish of rain is another – and how I did remains one of those things I often ponder over.

Twisting, swirling, sunfishing up to the topmost rails, and spinning down again, Midnight did his best. I did mine. We battled as we had many times before, and finally Midnight raised his head to walk quietly across to the mare.

When Bill handed me her lead rope, he said, "So help me, mate, how did you stay there? I shut my eyes when he went up on them rails."

I said, "It's gettin' so it's habit. Though one of these days I'll forget, an' he'll have me. So long, Bill, an' thanks for everything."

Bill called, "So long," and opened the gates to let me ride out.

Midnight strode forcibly, splattering mud in a long striding walk. Moonlight jogged by his side, serene, despite the torrential pourings which were beating over us.

For two or three hours the track we were following wound through flat, one-time dusty plains. Now they were great sheets of water, rippled and torn by the driving rain.

My concern as I rode, streaming wet in the saddle, was the river I would soon have to cross. If the bridge was still intact I would have little trouble. If it was damaged, only one course was left – swim the river, or turn back to Bill, who was running short of food. I felt that already I had imposed too much on his kindness. The gnawing thought was that he might be isolated and not get food for weeks if the rain kept on. And my being with him would aggravate, not help his situation.

When the timber-line of the river loomed through the scudding rain I had made up my mind, come what may, we had to cross. Midnight, I think, had done the same. He carried his ears pricked with eagerness, keen to get back to his home ground. But the possibilities looked grim as we neared the river's banks.

Normally sluggish, the river was tossing and boiling in flood. Instead of being thirty yards wide it was sixty or seventy, and still rising. Debris swirling in the current gave a good indication of this.

The bridge was awash, curled over with big cresting waves that looked frightening. And when I urged Midnight closer he snorted, warningly, stiffening the proud crest of his neck. Planting his fore-feet wide, he refused to be spurred on to the bridge's planking.

Knowing him, I said, "O.K. We'll see what it's like up stream."

No horse understands words, of course, but they sense inflection. Midnight wheeled and, with Moonlight jogging beside him, headed up river. We reached a bend, then paused in shallow muddy water while I stared to mid-stream.

For a moment I wavered. The current swirled and slid in a forbidding manner. The eddies seemed to be ribbed one

against the other. But Midnight shook his wet head impatiently, snatching at his bit for me to free him.

Thinking he might be of encouragement to Moonlight I slipped her rope around Midnight's neck then took two or three turns with the end. This allowed a fairly strong connection, yet one I could free quickly if needed.

And I remembered, numbed though I was in mind and body by the blinding pounding rain, noticing Moonlight's manner. She seemed oblivious of what storm, rain, and flood could do to her; as if greater things were encompassing her than the tortured swollen river.

She made no sound as Midnight nickered, striding strongly into the racing swirling flow. Soon he and Moonlight were shoulder deep, breasting into the deeper water. And suddenly I felt the pull as the current snatched at them both.

The snatch was so strong, and the smashing beat of rain so great, I had no sense of the horses swimming. Though their legs must have been driving with all the strength they possessed, I felt only the sucking boiling river pulling us on. It seemed I was smothering from water churned around from above and below.

Yet slowly but surely Midnight breasted his way against the torrent. Moonlight swam with him, keeping shoulder close to my knee, and sheltered to some extent by Midnight's powerful body.

When we were half-way between the bend and the bridge I judged we were heading fairly right; another thirty yards would diagonally bring us into shallow water, where the horses could fight for a footing.

But thirty yards in a roaring foaming river, ripped to frightening force by flood, seems unending. The blinding rain made judgement difficult, too, and when I glanced around to see a huge snag bearing down on us I thought the end had come.

But there is always a will that fights against extremities. The will this time was Midnight. From depths of strength known only to his wild tough spirit he surged forward taking Moonlight with him.

The snag swirled past, barely missing their tails. If ever a man felt his love for an animal grow to a greatness beyond words, I did at that moment. It's a memory I treasure from there and for all time.

We were closer to the broken bridge than I had estimated when the horses floundered to their feet. Luckily the bank was silted over with sand and not mud, which might have been a death trap.

Riding out from the seething reddish water, I patted Midnight's neck, then Moonlight's. They both shook their streaming heads, eager to be on the move again, so we rode on in the rain.

If anything it increased in force until everything seemed a sodden blur which was washing right through me. Then I felt Moonlight begin to drag on her rope. As if ordered, Midnight came to a stop and stood with his head to the rain while I slid from the soggy saddle.

Bush horses are not nurtured products of stables and veterinary surgeons. Their lives follow a cycle where birth and death are natural. Moonlight lay down on the soaked streaming ground and, without undue stress or strain, gave birth to a colt who, at first, didn't like the world he was born into. But after a puzzled sniff or two he scrambled up with his mother, to stand shivering wetly by her side. She licked his ears then, despite the rain, licked some semblance of warmth into his tiny hopeful body. Midnight whinnied, excited – as geldings always are – to see a new foal wobbling near him.

Numbed more than ever, I had to decide what to do. Moonlight could travel on, but the colt couldn't. His little legs and hooves would take several hours to strengthen, and I still had about ten miles to go. Scuffing water from my face I decided to attempt the impossible – put the little chap up in front of my saddle and hope Midnight wouldn't throw the two of us.

As I have said, Midnight was a strange horse. A mixture of brumbie and outlaw blood made him dangerous, and no one else had ever ridden him except me. Yet he stood like a rock while I slid the colt on to his withers, then mounted.

For an awful chilled moment I thought he was going to buck – throw the colt and me if he could, into the rain-splashed puddles. Then he stepped out smartly, bearing us both without effort. Moonlight strode with him, pacing step for step. From there on the miles were a rain-drenched curtain through which we had to pass.

Reaching the homestead I shut Moonlight and her foal in a stall where straw was fetlock deep. Hay, too, hung from the pine wall racks.

Midnight I turned loose. He was that kind of horse – no softness; no gentleness; just sheer hard endurance, bred to all kinds of weather.

And as he splashed away, whinnying for his mates somewhere out in the darkness, I remembered the river. Only a horse of Midnight's calibre could have borne me across it. And only Midnight knew the closeness of Moonlight's need.

Is it any wonder that I loved him?

A RIDE WITH MARK

K. M. PEYTON

from Flambards

Christina has been sent to live with relatives at their house, Flambards. Mark, her arrogant cousin, is considered to be an ideal match for her, but Christina has formed a stronger friendship with Dick, the groom.

CHRISTINA LAY LOOKING at the moon, thinking of the long years ahead of her in the troubled atmosphere of Flambards. "It's better than an orphanage," she thought. And Mark would make a very handsome husband. And then, suddenly she remembered Dick, dear, kind Dick who was always nice to her, and she thought, "What a pity I can't marry Dick."

Two days later Mark took her out. She rode Sweetbriar and Mark rode Treasure, his favourite, who was nervous and sweating. Dick led the horses out and held Sweetbriar while Christina got into the saddle. He held her stirrup for her, patted the mare's neck and said softly, "Have a good ride, miss."

Christina wanted to tell that she would rather be going with him, but decided it would be out of place. Dick went to Mark, to tighten Treasure's girths, and the horse stood for him, flitching his long, nervous ears. Mark looked down on Dick from the saddle and said, "Don't be all day." He wore a black jacket and black cap, and sat very easily, his reins all in one hand. Christina felt worried, and tried to sit her best, and look confident.

"Come on," Mark said.

Sweetbriar moved off to Christina's heel, and Treasure pranced past her, rattling his bit, a white rim showing round his eyes. Mark turned in his saddle and laughed. "What a horse, eh? You wouldn't think he galloped ten miles yesterday, would you? I reckon Father's right when he says he'll be winning races in a year or two's time."

Christina nudged Sweetbriar into a trot to keep up, and Mark watched her critically.

"Sit square, hands still. That's better."

Unaccountably, Christina felt furious, although she had never minded Dick's instruction. She stared crossly between Sweetbriar's ears and wondered why Mark let Treasure proceed at a crabwise jogging pace, instead of making him walk or trot properly. From Dick, she had learnt that this was a bad habit in a horse, but Mark, allowing bad habits himself, criticized her. Christina raged, her lips tight.

"Not bad," Mark said. "Let's see you canter."

Treasure was off at a bound, fighting his bit, the sweat gathering on his neck. Christina had to admit that Mark sat him beautifully, very strong and yet graceful in the saddle, completely master of the difficult horse. She let Sweetbriar go, dear Sweetbriar whom she could always trust to look after her – and the mare went easily, light on her bit, ignoring the headstrong youngster raking along at her side, fighting for his head.

"Why, you're not bad at all," Mark shouted, sounding quite surprised, and Christina's anger changed to a hot glow of pride. She did not let her expression change, but thought, "Nice Dick. You are all right, I've saved you."

She steadied Sweetbriar as they came to a gate, and Mark

brought Treasure to a halt with a cruel pressure on the curb.

"Honestly, he's a mad horse," Mark said. "You wait here, and I'll show you what he can do, get the tickle out of his toes. He'll be all right when he's run it off a bit."

He turned Treasure sharply on his hocks and went off at a fast canter away from Christina across the field. Christina watched him go, glad that Sweetbriar was content to stand, mildly switching her ears to the winter crying of the rooks. Mark made for a low part of the cut and laid fence and Treasure flew it with scarcely a change in his stride, and continued at a gallop across the field beyond.

"Show-off," Christina thought. She had never been left alone on a horse before. The air was cold and clear, and she felt confident. She looked down at her gloved hands on the reins, quiet and firm, and the frosted neck of the mare shining with her two hours' daily polishing. She thought of the spotless stables, and the great feeds the horses got, and wondered if Dick and the others lived in anything like the same luxury as the horses they cared for. Dick, in spite of his stocky frame, was thinner than he should be, and had been coughing recently. If a horse coughed, it was rested and given stuff out of a bottle and invalid gruel with an egg beaten in it, but when Christina had said to Dick, "You ought to stay by a fire with a cough like that," he looked at her in amazement and said, "But I couldn't stay off work, miss." "Why not?" Christina had asked, but Dick had only laughed, rather bitterly. Christina thought, "I ought to know about the servants. I don't know anything." She thought that when you lived in a big house in the country, you were supposed to go round and give food and clothes to the poor, but how could she do it when she was the poor herself? Her thoughts had wandered far away from Mark and Treasure by the time they reappeared, still galloping, back over the cut and laid fence and, more soberly, back to Sweetbriar's side. Mark's eyes were sparkling.

"There, that's satisfied him, eh? He'll go easily enough now."

Treasure certainly looked quieter, breathing easily through his distended nostrils. He was in superb condition, his coat gleaming like the dining-room mahogany.

"Look, you ought to try him," Mark said. "You've never ridden a proper horse yet. I don't know what Dick's thinking of."

"What do you mean, a proper horse?" Christina said indignantly. "What's wrong with Sweetbriar?"

"You know what I mean," Mark said. They were walking side by side across the field to the gate in the corner.

"You ought to ride all sorts. You'd feel a difference, I can tell you."

"I don't want to ride Treasure."

"Are you afraid?" Mark asked cruelly, smiling.

"No, of course not. But if Dick thought I was up to riding Treasure he would probably have let me by now."

"Oh Dick, Dick, Dick! He's only a servant. What does he know? Don't be so stupid. Come on, I'll change the saddles over for you, and you try him. I tell you, it'll be an experience for you – you'll be able to tell Father."

Christina hesitated. She felt doubtful about riding Treasure, but not afraid. Mark pulled up. "Come on. You ought to be jolly proud I'll let you."

Christina had no alternative but to get down. She held the horses while Mark changed the saddles over, then Mark gave her a leg up on to Treasure.

"Oh, all these reins!" Christina said, confused. She felt nervous now, looking at the very different neck in front of her, and the white rim of Treasure's eye.

"Look, you should learn. These are the snaffle reins, and these the curb. You hold them like this." He showed her. "There, that's right."

He mounted Sweetbriar, and looked at her critically. "Don't jab him with the curb, or he'll show you he doesn't like it."

Christina did not feel very happy. She was not afraid, she told herself. But Treasure was all spirit. Even as he walked, she could feel it inside him; it quivered in her fingers as he tossed his head, pulling at the reins. He started to dance, moving along at the jog, instead of a walk. Mark laughed. Suddenly a gun went off in the woods behind them and Treasure gave a great leap forward. Christina, carried by the pommel beneath her thighs, was lifted with him, not even losing a stirrup. She heard Mark laugh again, and cry, "Hold him! Hold him!" But Treasure did not want to be held. He reached out his neck and pulled the reins through her fingers, and then he was galloping, and Christina knew that she was on her own.

She was not afraid, immediately. The sheer exhilaration of the horse's speed thrilled her, but his strength was ominous. When she looked down she saw his shoulders moving with the smooth rhythm of steam—pistons; she saw his black, shining hoofs thrown out, thudding the hard turf, and felt the great eagerness coming up through her own body. She knew that she could never stop him, if he decided he did not want to stop. She saw the hedge ahead of them, and the first stab of real fear contracted her stomach. She gathered her reins up tight, and pulled hard. It made no difference at all.

"Don't panic," she thought, but the panic was in her, whether she wanted it or not.

Treasure's stride lengthened as he approached the hedge. Christina, remembering William, shut her eyes and buried her hands in Treasure's mane, and the horse surged beneath her. There was a cracking noise of breaking twigs. Christina gasped, clutched and gasped again, but to her amazement they were galloping again, the incident behind them, and she still in place. She let go of Treasure's mane and pulled on his mouth again, with all her strength, but he had the bit firmly between his teeth and she could make no impression. A great despair filled her.

"I shall be killed ," she thought.

Treasure was turning right-handed across another large, yellow field. Beyond it was the home paddock where Christina had taken her safe, enjoyable lessons with Dick. It dawned on her that the horse was making for home, but between the field they were in and the home paddock there was a hedge, very much larger than the one they had just jumped, solid and newly layered all along its length, and a good five feet high. Christina knew that Treasure was not the horse to be stopped by such an obstacle; she knew that he was going to jump it, and, by the grace of God, so was she. A great sob of despair broke from her throat.

"Treasure, don't! Don't, don't!" She leaned back on the reins, trying to saw them in the horse's mouth, but she could do nothing.

The creak of leather beneath her, the heavy thrumming of the horse's hoofs, filled her ears, which ached with the cold wind. Her hair flew behind her. The horse, never tiring, galloped on, raking out with his flying hoofs.

Suddenly, in the mist of her watery vision, Christina saw a grey horse come into sight at the top of the field. It was cantering towards her, but circling slightly in such a way that it looked as if it would come round and join her on her own headlong course. Christina thought it was Mark, impossibly flown to save her. She lifted her head, and screamed into the wind, "Help me! Please help me!" The hedge was getting rapidly closer, and she started to cry out with fear, half-sob, half-entreaty. Treasure's strength grew with every stride.

The grey horse, very much under control, had now circled so that he was on the same course as her, but ahead and to her right. As Treasure galloped on, the grey horse's stride lengthened to match, and quite suddenly Treasure was galloping with his nose close by the grey horse's side.

They were both galloping, and Christina heard a voice shout, "Hold tight, Miss Christina!" The grey was hard against Treasure's shoulders, its rider's legs crushed against the horse's wild movement. Treasure was forced off course, ridden off by the grey, and Dick was leaning over to take the reins, his face puckered with anxiety.

"Hold hard!"

Christina felt the horses sliding, skidding, the great gallop broken up into a series of jolts and crashes, Treasure berserk beneath her. Strips of turf peeled up under his hoofs. Dick was pulled up out of his saddle, and hung for a moment, precariously straddled between the two horses, then at last Treasure dropped his jaw and pulled up and Dick, still holding on, half fell and half jumped from his saddle, staggering and swearing.

"You great ruddy brute! You devil you!" But as Treasure pulled up he was stroking his neck, gentling him and swearing at the same time; then he came round to Christina's side and lifted her down. Christina's legs had no strength in them and she stumbled against him.

"Dick! Oh, Dick!" she wept, and Dick tried to comfort her, with Treasure plunging round in circles on one hand, and Woodpigeon, the grey, sidling about on the other. He was full of indignation.

"Oh, Miss Christina, he shouldn't ever have put you on Treasure. He must be out of his mind. Steady on, my old beauty!" – this to Treasure, who was now beginning to quieten – "And you riding not a couple of months yet! There, miss, it's all right now."

Being spoken to as if she were a horse had a soothing effect on Christina, and she found that she was able to stand without her knees shaking. She wiped the mud and tears off her face and looked round dubiously.

"It was very clever of you to stop him, Dick," she said. The thorn hedge was some thirty yards away, and even nastier than she had supposed. There was a big drainage ditch on the take-off, newly-dug, with the earth thrown out all along its lip. "What do you think would have happened if – ?" Christina's knees started shaking again. "I don't think I shall like hunting," she said. She thought of having to report to Uncle Russell that she had funked the big hedges and gone through the gates, and Mark would tell him that she was no good.

"Only a fool would put at a hedge like that, miss, even out hunting. You mustn't get afraid now, because of this. You sat him a treat. There, my old fellow, my old boy. You take it easy now." He had Treasure quite quiet, lipping at his fingers. "This horse isn't bad, miss. He's only young. He needs steady riding, not like he gets with Mr Mark."

"Where is Mark?" Christina said.

"Coming now, miss."

Christina was furious with Mark, now that her fright was over. Mark cantered slowly up on Sweetbriar, looking very unconcerned. But when he pulled up beside them and looked at them both, Christina could see that he was afraid, and angry, but did not want it to show. He laughed and said to Christina, "Well, how about that for a gallop? Did you enjoy it?"

"He'd have gone through that hedge if Dick hadn't stopped him," Christina said coldly. "Then where would I have been?"

"Home by now," Mark said flippantly.

"She could have been killed, sir, and you know it," Dick said suddenly. "You had no right to put her on this horse."

"So you're taking credit for saving her life?" Mark said, his face flushing angrily.

"No. But I reckon it was lucky Mr Fowler told me to take Woodpigeon out for an hour, that's all."

Mark got down from Sweetbriar and said to Dick abruptly, "Change the saddles back."

Dick did as he was told, silently. When Sweetbriar was ready he gave Christina a leg up, and Christina settled herself gratefully on the mare, and said, very gravely, "Thank you very much, Dick." She loved Dick very much at that moment, and hated Mark with a cold, flat contempt. Dick looked up at her and smiled one of his rare, sweet smiles.

"That's all right, miss."

Mark said to him, "Hold Treasure while I mount."

Dick soothed the bay horse, who sensed Mark's anger and was nervous again. When Mark had gathered up his reins, he paused and looked down at Dick.

"You won't mention what happened, when you get back?"

Dick said nothing. Mark flushed again, his anger rising.

"You heard what I said? No one is to know what happened."

"If you say so, sir."

"Look," said Mark, very gently, "I do say so. And I'll say something else. If I find out that anyone in the stables knows what happened this morning, I'll see that you get dismissed."

Dick's eyes opened very wide. He stroked Treasure's neck, silent, turning away from Christina.

"Well?"

"Yes, sir," Dick said. "I understand."

STRAWBERRY'S ADVENTURE

C. S. LEWIS

from The Magician's Nephew

After several adventures, Digory (whose mother is very ill) and Polly have found themselves in the magical kingdom of Narnia which is ruled by a lion, Aslan. Also in Narnia are a horse, Strawberry, and his owners – a cab driver and his wife who have been crowned king and queen. Aslan is angry with Digory for accidentally bringing the evil Witch to Narnia.

DIGORY KEPT HIS MOUTH very tight shut. He had been growing more and more uncomfortable. He hoped that, whatever happened, he wouldn't blub or do anything ridiculous.

"Son of Adam," said Aslan. "Are you ready to undo the wrong that you have done to my sweet country of Narnia on the very day of its birth?"

"Well, I don't see what I can do," said Digory. "You see, the Witch ran away and – "

"I asked, are you ready?" said the Lion.

"Yes," said Digory. He had had for a second some wild idea of saying "I'll try to help you if you'll promise to help about my Mother", but he realized in time that the Lion was not at all the sort of person one could try to make bargains with. But when he had said "Yes", he thought of his Mother, and he thought of the great hopes he had had, and how they were all dying away, and a lump came in his throat and tears in his eyes, and he blurted out:

"But please, please – won't you – can't you give me something that will cure Mother?" Up till then he had been looking at the Lion's great front feet and the huge claws on them; now, in his despair, he looked up at its face. What he saw surprised him as much as anything in his whole life. For the tawny face was bent down near his own and (wonder of wonders) great shining tears stood in the Lion's eyes. They were such big, bright tears compared with Digory's own that for a moment he felt as if the Lion must really be sorrier about his Mother than he was himself.

"My son, my son," said Aslan. "I know. Grief is great. Only you and I in this land know that yet. Let us be good to one another. But I have to think of hundreds of years in the life of Narnia. The Witch whom you have brought into this world will come back to Narnia again. But it need not be yet. It is my wish to plant in Narnia a tree that she will not dare to approach, and that tree will protect Narnia from her for many years. So this land shall have a long, bright morning before any clouds come over the sun. You must get me the seed from which that tree is to grow."

"Yes, sir," said Digory. He didn't know how it was to be done but he felt quite sure now that he would be able to do it. The Lion drew a deep breath, stooped its head even lower and gave him a Lion's kiss. And at once Digory felt that new strength and courage had gone into him.

"Dear son," said Aslan, "I will tell you what you must do. Turn and look to the West and tell me what do you see?"

"I see terribly big mountains, Aslan," said Digory. "I see this river coming down cliffs in a waterfall. And beyond the cliff there are high green hills with forests. And beyond those there are higher ranges that look almost black. And then, far, far away, there are big snowy mountains all heaped up together – like pictures of the Alps. And behind those there's nothing but the sky."

"You see well," said the Lion. "Now the land of Narnia ends where the waterfall comes down, and once you have reached the top of the cliff you will be out of Narnia and into the Western Wild. You must journey through those mountains till you find a green valley with a blue lake in it, walled round by mountains of ice. At the end of the lake there is a steep, green hill. On the top of that hill there is a garden. In the centre of that garden is a tree. Pluck an apple from that tree and bring it back to me."

"Yes, sir," said Digory again. He hadn't the least idea of how he was to climb the cliff and find his way among all the mountains, but he didn't like to say that for fear it would sound like making excuses. But he did say, "I hope, Aslan, you're not in a hurry. I shan't be able to get there and back very quickly."

"Little son of Adam, you shall have help," said Aslan. He then turned to the Horse who had been standing quietly beside them all this time, swishing his tail to keep the flies off, and listening with his head on one side as if the conversation were a little difficult to understand.

"My dear," said Aslan to the Horse, "would you like to be a winged horse?"

You should have seen how the Horse shook its mane and how its nostrils widened, and the little tap it gave the ground with one back hoof. Clearly it would very much like to be a winged horse. But it only said:

"If you wish, Aslan – if you really mean – I don't know why it should be me – I'm not a very clever horse."

"Be winged. Be the father of all flying horses," roared Aslan in a voice that shook the ground. "Your name is Fledge."

The horse shied, just as it might have shied in the old, miserable days when it pulled a hansom. Then it reared. It strained its neck back as if there were a fly biting its shoulders and it wanted to scratch them. And then, just as the beasts had burst out of the earth, there burst out from

78

the shoulders of Fledge wings that spread and grew, larger
than eagles', larger than swans', larger than angels' wings
in church windows. The feathers shone chestnut colour and
copper colour. He gave a great sweep with them and
leaped into the air. Twenty feet above Aslan and Digory he
snorted, neighed, and curvetted. Then, after circling once
round them, he dropped to the earth, all four hoofs
together, looking awkward and surprised, but extremely
pleased.

"Is it good, Fledge?" said Aslan.

"It is very good, Aslan," said Fledge.

"Will you carry this little son of Adam on your back to the mountain-valley I spoke of?"

"What? Now? At once?" said Strawberry – or Fledge, as we must now call him – "Hurrah! Come on little one. I've had things like you on my back before. Long, long ago. When there were green fields; and sugar."

"What are the two daughters of Eve whispering about?" said Aslan, turning very suddenly on Polly and the Cabby's wife, who had in fact been making friends.

"If you please, sir," said Queen Helen (for that is what Nellie the cabman's wife now was), "I think the little girl would love to go too, if it weren't no trouble."

"What does Fledge say about that?" asked the Lion.

"Oh, I don't mind two, not when they're little ones," said Fledge. "But I hope the Elephant doesn't want to come as well."

The Elephant had no such wish, and the new King of Narnia helped both the children up: that is, he gave Digory a rough heave and set Polly as gently and daintily on the horse's back as if she were made of china and might break. "There they are, Strawberry – Fledge, I should say, This is a rum go."

"Do not fly too high," said Aslan. "Do not try to go over the tops of the great ice—mountains. Look out for the valleys, the green places and fly through them. There will always be a way through. And now, begone with my blessing."

"Oh Fledge!" said Digory, leaning forward to pat the Horse's glossy neck. "This is fun. Hold on to me tight, Polly."

Next moment the country dropped away beneath them, and whirled round as Fledge, like a huge pigeon, circled once or twice before setting off on his long westward flight. Looking down, Polly could hardly see the King and the Queen, and even Aslan himself was only a bright yellow spot on the green grass. Soon the wind was in their faces and Fledge's wings settled down to a steady beat.

All Narnia, many-coloured with lawns and rocks and heather and different sorts of trees, lay spread out below them, the river winding through it like a ribbon of quicksilver. They could already see over the tops of the low hills which lay northward on their right; beyond those hills a great moorland sloped gently up and up to the horizon.

On their left the mountains were much higher, but every now and then there was a gap where you could see, between steep pine woods, a glimpse of the southern lands that lay beyond them, looking blue and far away.

"That'll be where Archenland is," said Polly.

"Yes, but look ahead!" said Digory.

For now a great barrier of cliffs rose before them and they were almost dazzled by the sunlight dancing on the great waterfall by which the river roars and sparkles down into Narnia itself from the high western lands in which it rises. They were flying so high already that the thunder of those falls could only just be heard as a small, thin sound, but they were not yet high enough to fly over the top of the cliffs.

"We'll have to do a bit of zig—zagging here," said Fledge. "Hold on tight."

He began flying to and fro, getting higher at each turn. The air grew colder, and they heard the call of eagles far below them.

"I say, look back! Look behind," said Polly.

There they could see the whole valley of Narnia stretched out to where, just before the eastern horizon, there was a gleam of the sea. And now they were so high that they could see tiny—looking jagged mountains appearing beyond the northern moors, and plains of what looked like sand far in the south.

"I wish we had someone to tell us what all those places are," said Digory.

"I don't suppose they're anywhere yet," said Polly. "I mean, there's no one there, and nothing happening. The world only began today."

"No, but people will get there," said Digory. "And then they'll have histories, you know."

"Well, it's a jolly good thing they haven't now," said Polly. "Because nobody can be made to learn it. Battles and dates and all that rot."

Now they were over the top of the cliffs and in a few

minutes the valley-land of Narnia had sunk out of sight behind them. They were flying over a wild country of steep hills and dark forests, still following the course of the river. The really big mountains loomed ahead. But the sun was now in the travellers' eyes and they couldn't see things very clearly in that direction. For the sun sank lower and lower till the western sky was all like one great furnace full of melted gold; and it set at last behind a jagged peak which stood up against the brightness as sharp and flat as if it were cut out of cardboard.

"It's none too warm up here," said Polly.

"And my wings are beginning to ache," said Fledge.

"There's no sign of the valley with a lake in it, like what Aslan said. What about coming down and looking out for a decent spot to spend the night in? We shan't reach that place tonight."

"Yes, and surely it's about time for supper?" said Digory.

So Fledge came lower and lower. As they came down nearer to the earth and among the hills, the air grew warmer; and after travelling so many hours with nothing to listen to but the beat of Fledge's wings, it was nice to hear the homely and earthy noises again – the chatter of the river on its stony bed and the creaking of trees in the light wind. A warm, good smell of sun-baked earth and grass and flowers came up to them. At last Fledge alighted. Digory rolled off and helped Polly to dismount. Both were glad to stretch their stiff legs.

The valley in which they had come down was in the heart of the mountains; snowy heights, one of them looking rose-red in the reflection of the sunset, towered above them.

"I am hungry," said Digory.

"Well, tuck in," said Fledge, taking a big mouthful of grass. Then he raised his head, still chewing and with bits of grass sticking out on each side of his mouth like whiskers, and said, "Come on, you two. Don't be shy. There's plenty for us all."

"But we can't eat grass," said Digory.

"H'm, h'm," said Fledge, speaking with his mouth full. "Well – h'm – don't know quite what you'll do then. Very good grass too."

Polly and Digory stared at one another in dismay.

"Well, I do think someone might have arranged about our meals," said Digory.

"I'm sure Aslan would have, if you'd asked him," said Fledge.

"Wouldn't he know without being asked?" said Polly.

"I've no doubt he would," said the Horse (still with his mouth full). "But I've a sort of idea he likes to be asked."

"But what on earth are we to do?" asked Digory.

"I'm sure I don't know," said Fledge. "Unless you try the grass. You might like it better than you think."

"Oh, don't be silly," said Polly, stamping her foot. "Of course humans can't eat grass, any more than you could eat a mutton chop."

"For goodness' sake don't talk about chops and things," said Digory. "It only makes it worse."

Digory said that Polly had better take herself home by ring and get something to eat there: he couldn't himself because he had promised to go straight on his message for Aslan, and, if once he showed up again at home, anything might happen to prevent his getting back. But Polly said she wouldn't leave him, and Digory said it was jolly decent of her.

"I say," said Polly, "I've still got the remains of that bag of toffee in my pocket. It'll be better than nothing."

"A lot better," said Digory. "But be careful to get your hand into your pocket without touching your ring."

This was a difficult and delicate job but they managed it in the end. The little paper bag was very squashy and sticky when they finally got it out, so that it was more a question of tearing the bag off the toffees than of getting the toffees out of the bag. Some grown-ups (you know how fussy they can be about that sort of thing) would rather have gone without supper altogether than eaten those toffees. There were nine of them all told. It was Digory who had the bright idea of eating four each and planting the ninth; for, as he said, "if the bar off the lamp-post turned into a little light-tree, why shouldn't this turn into a toffee-tree?" So they dibbled a small hole in the turf and buried the piece of toffee. Then they ate the other pieces, making them last as long as they could. It was a poor meal, even with all the paper they couldn't help eating as well.

When Fledge had quite finished his own excellent supper he lay down. The children came and sat one on each side of him leaning against his warm body, and when he had spread a wing over each they were really quite snug.

As the bright young stars of that new world came out they talked over everything: how Digory had hoped to get something for his Mother and how, instead of that, he had been sent on this message. And they repeated to one another all the signs by which they would know the place they were looking for – the blue lake and the hill with a garden on top of it. The talk was just beginning to slow down as they got sleepy, when suddenly Polly sat up wide awake and said "Hush!"

Everyone listened as hard as they could.

"Perhaps it was only the wind in the trees," said Digory presently.

"I'm not so sure," said Fledge. "Anyway – wait! There it goes again. By Aslan, it is something."

The horse scrambled to its feet with a great noise and a great upheaval; the children were already on theirs. Fledge trotted to and fro, sniffing and whinnying. The children tip-toed this way and that, looking behind every bush and tree. They kept on thinking they saw things, and there was one time when Polly was perfectly certain she had seen a tall, dark figure gliding quickly away in a westerly direction. But they caught nothing and in the end Fledge lay down again and the children re-snuggled (if that is the right word) under his wings. They went to sleep at once. Fledge stayed awake much longer moving his ears to and fro in the darkness and sometimes giving a little shiver with his skin as if a fly had lighted on him: but in the end he too slept.

A GAUCHO IN THE PAMPA

A. F. TSCHIFFELY

OH YES, I REMEMBER him so well that he seems to be standing before me as I'm writing these lines. He was a lovely chap, a golden-red and snow-white skewbald with a bristly mane, proud fiery eyes and a long flowing tail. Where he was bought, and how much he cost, I never bothered to ask; not out of politeness, for in those days of my early childhood I didn't know that one mustn't look a gift horse in the mouth. When first I laid eyes on him, my joy was so great that I forgot everything else; my greatest desire was fulfilled: I owned a horse! What a wonderful beast he was; his manners were perfect, and despite the somewhat wild look in his eyes, he was so quiet and docile that alongside him even the proverbially quiet lamb would have been frisky.

After my father had lifted me onto his back, he stood stock-still, and only moved a little when I gingerly urged him to do so. Finding that he wasn't "flighty", as some Irish horsemen say, I gradually became more confident, and, letting him have his head, made him jog along merrily. The thrill of it; my father, mother, sisters and brother looking on as I showed off, sitting on my horse! From that moment on, he and I became inseparable friends, and unless some interfering grown-up person dragged me away from him when it was time to eat or to go to bed, I enjoyed every moment of his company.

With constant practice, and thanks to my elder brother's instructions, I soon became a tolerably good rider, and as my confidence grew, I even risked a gallop. For a few moments the excitement was such that I held my breath, but upon finding my balance I gave vent to my feelings, screaming with joy. Even my pal, a black poodle, joined in the fun, but when jumping to give one of my legs a playful nip, he met with an accident which caused quite a commotion. As bad luck would have it, one of his paws got under the horse, and the poor dog's howls and yelps of pain were such that half the household rushed to the scene to see what was amiss. Fortunately, no serious harm had been done, and after the affected paw had been stroked by sympathetic hands, he once more wagged his tail, but later took good care to keep at a distance when any riding was being done.

My brother often asked me to lend him my horse, and when this was refused, or he simply "bagged" him without my permission, this led to serious rows, and occasionally even fights, of which I – being the younger of the two – invariably got the worst. Here I must relate that this went on for some time, until, one day, to my amazement I discovered that he was by no means invincible, whereafter all fighting between the two of us ceased. But that's another story, so let's go back to my horse.

Every morning and evening, and sometimes several times during the day, I groomed him with great care, with the result that his coat had a gloss like a mirror. He never did anything wrong, and if ever a slight accident happened, it was always my fault. He never bucked, stumbled, kicked, bit or bolted, and had it not been that my mother objected, he could easily have been taken into the drawing-room where he would have behaved himself every bit as well as our poodle who usually was allowed to go into that room, filled with frail furniture, fancy china, delicate vases and all sorts of fragile nick-nacks I was hardly allowed to look at, let alone touch. Between ourselves, I hated that beastly drawing-room, and only went into it when, after having been washed and scrubbed until the skin of my face nearly cracked, I had to go to say "How d'you do?" to visitors, whereafter I fairly bolted back to my beloved horse. When sitting on him, I was the happiest boy in the world. As I cantered along, I imagined being a Red Indian Chief, or a general dashing into battle. In those days I didn't know that modern generals only bestride horses when they are on parade, and that whilst the armies under their command are at close grips with the enemy, they are usually far away from the battlefields, receiving telephone and wireless messages which cause them to consult large-scale wall-maps. Then, again, I imagined being a tamer of wild horses, riding a wicked bucking bronco, or I saw myself in a circus ring, putting a high school horse through his paces. Of course, if I was a jockey riding in a race, my invincible mount always led the field, and if it was a point-to-point we were running, no obstacle was too stiff for my trusty steed, which fairly sailed over them without ever putting a hoof wrong.

One day, when I was about to mount in order to indulge in such a flight of fancy, my brother tried to take my horse from me, During the ensuing struggle for possession, he pulled at my pet's head, whilst I tugged in the opposite direction, holding on to his tail, which suddenly came out, with the result that I fell over backwards. When I rose, still holding the beautiful tail in my hands, and realized the magnitude of the disaster, I cried bitterly, and even after the tail had been replaced with the help of glue, I felt my darling rocking-horse would never be the same again.

Several years passed, and I had forgotten all about the joy of my early childhood when, one day I made a voyage

of exploration up into the attic. There, among broken chairs, old picture frames, toys, trunks, hand-bags, pots and pans, and all sorts of odds and ends, some of which brought back various memories, was my dear old rocking-horse, covered with dust and cobwebs. Taking a piece of rag, I carefully wiped him down, and as I did so, his fiery eyes looked at me, as if in reproach. One of his legs being broken, I carried him into the gardener's shed for repairs, and a few days later, when the glue had dried, I saw the last of my formerly inseparable companion when he was taken to a jumble sale.

As I grew older, I did a great deal of riding, but it was only when I went to live in South America that, for the first time in my life, I became the owner of a real live horse. Now I'll relate how this came about, and introduce you to the remarkable animal I bought.

I was having a grand time out in the Pampa, as the

immense Argentine plain is called. *Pampa* is an old Indian word, meaning "space"; and a perfect name it is for the seemingly endless expanse of grass and sky. We had been rounding up cattle, and were slowly cantering home, seated on our sweating stock ponies, when a dark patch on the distant horizon attracted our attention. My companions were six or eight *gauchos* – as cowboys are called in the Argentine – and after they had slowed down in order to see better, all agreed that what we were observing in the distance was a troop of horses being driven in our direction.

Shortly after we had reached the ranch, and our ponies had been washed down and turned loose, some thirty tired horses, led by a bell mare, halted near the corral, and when we went to see who might be the men in charge of them, found that all were strangers who had driven the troop for hundreds of miles across the Pampa. It was a bunch of fine animals they had brought, all sturdy and of various colours; but one, a piebald, despite being thin and bedraggled, particularly attracted my attention. The animals were to be sold in a little town situated some fifty miles from the ranch, and as they, as well as the herdsmen, showed the effects of so long and arduous a journey, they were invited to remain with us until the cattle and horse sale was to be held. The piebald of my fancy was deep-chested and stood just a shade under fifteen hands, and judging by his appearance and movements, even a greenhorn could have told that he must be tough and nimble.

Ever since my early childhood, when I was the proud owner of the skewbald rocking-horse, I have had a liking for animals of "broken" colours; that is to say, those with patches and blotches of brown, golden-red or black, irregularly arranged on white. Probably this is why I immediately took a fancy to the newly arrived piebald whose peculiar black patches made him look like a circus horse.

After having allowed the horses to graze and rest for three days, they were rounded up once more, and driven into the corral, this time to be tested for riding. Some had never been saddled, so we had great fun, and no little excitement, mounting them for the first time. How they bucked, kicked and even squealed with rage! However, it was of no avail; the riders stuck on as if glued to the animals. The piebald of my fancy happened to be tame, and very well broken in, so when I took him for an outing, he behaved perfectly. He galloped and cantered so smoothly I was hardly aware of the speed at which he travelled, and where the ground was rough and uneven, or full of holes, he never hesitated nor slackened his pace, but fairly glided along.

Whilst cantering back to the corral, I made up my mind to buy the horse, but realizing that, most likely, his owner would put a high price on him, I decided to be cunning about my proposed deal. Accordingly, when I dismounted, and was asked what was my opinion of the piebald, I merely shrugged my shoulders and replied, "not bad".

But to make a long story short; that very evening, after the usual haggling, I paid the equivalent of ten pounds for him, and from that moment on he was mine. Having completed the deal, I went to catch the animal, and soon after was busy grooming him and trimming his hoofs. As usual in the Pampa, none of the horses was shod, shoes being unnecessary in those regions where stones and rocks are practically nowhere to be seen. It felt grand to be grooming my own animal which appeared to be enjoying tnese attentions, especially when I vigorously brushed him under the chin or behind his ears. Since his arrival he had already put on a bit of flesh, and when I finished the job, and stepped back a few paces to have a good look at him, I was very pleased. On either side of his face was a large black patch, and the top of his broad forehead and short ever-alert ears were of the same colour. From his throat down to his chest he had a marking resembling an apron, and, his four extremities being black, he appeared to be wearing beautifully polished top-boots. Then, of course, he had large black patches and blotches all over his body which, after having been groomed, fairly glistened in the late evening sun. He kept on looking towards the place where his companions were grazing in the plain resembling an ocean in which the ranch and its surrounding trees appeared to be a solitary island. Every now and again he neighed, calling his friends, and when,

after he had eaten a good ration of crushed oats, I turned him loose, he raised his head and tail, and raced towards them.

After darkness had fallen, and the whole of nature seemed to be at peace and resting, we were sitting round a roaring fire over which two sheep's sides were being roasted on iron spears stuck into the round. When the meat was ready, out of leather sheaths that were stuck in every gaucho's wide coin-studded belt were drawn knives with which ribs and pieces of meat were dextrously cut of the roast. No plates or forks were used, but the men daintily held the meat between the tips of their thumbs and forefingers of one hand, whilst cutting with the other, and they were so clever at doing this that only the two finger-tips got slightly greasy.

After the meal, when the owner of the recently arrived horses had retired for the night, his men, some of our ranch hands and I, continued to sit near the fire, smoking and talking about people and happenings. When the conversation changed to the inevitable subject, namely horses, one of the visitors, a wiry, sun-tanned and grey-haired old gaucho, turned towards me and slowly asked in a deep bass voice:

"Señor, how do you like the piebald you bought today?"

This time there was no need for me to be foxy, as had been the case after I had ridden the animal for the first time, and I hoped to buy him cheaply; so I frankly replied that I thought my acquisition had the makings of a very good mount.

"Yes," the old gaucho said, at the same time nodding his assent, and then continued, "you've picked the best of the bunch. Just wait until he has rested and fed for another month or so, and then you'll see. He's one of the toughest mustangs I've ever known, and if you're interested, I'll tell you a story about him."

"Please do," I and several listeners said in chorus; so when the old centaur had lit another cigarette, he began:

94

"Your piebald comes from a region situated in the far South, near the cordillera. Some time ago, an outlaw named Luna repeatedly attacked travellers, and even had the audacity to make single-handed raids on ranches. He was a killer, and as cunning as a puma, and although once or twice he was cornered, he managed to slip away into the mountain where no one could track him down. On several occasions, when his pursuers were hot on his heels, thanks to an amazingly swift and untiring horse he had stolen, he always outdistanced them. Chasing a desperado through those wild rocky valleys is a tough and dangerous proposition, for even if a pursuer happens to be mounted on an animal which is used to travelling fast over such difficult ground, a well-aimed bullet from an ambush is likely to end the chase. Anyway, although several expeditions set out into the mountain wilderness to capture Luna, dead or alive, all failed, and when we thought he had vanished to some other region, he suddenly reappeared to renew his murderous assaults. One day, little half-caste Indian policeman – not much of a chap to look at in his old tattered and patched-up uniform which once upon a time had been brown – turned up on an old nag. He hardly spoke to anyone, but after having nosed around a corral in which horses happened to be shut up, he asked their owner to lend him one he fancied for the job of tracking down the outlaw. Everybody was surprised when the little policeman said that he intended to go alone, and great was our astonishment when, with a number of excellent horses to choose from, he picked the piebald you bought today. Early next morning, as we watched him jog away in the direction of the bleak snow-capped mountains, all of us felt certain that this was the last we would see of him. Days passed, and after three weeks, when we thought the inevitable had happened to the lone man-hunter, he reappeared on your piebald, calmly leading Luna's famous horse by a length of rope. Fastened to the latter animal's riderless saddle was a small bundle made of a pair of trousers, and when this was opened, it was found to contain Luna's head. Having handed back to its owner the horse he had been lent, the feline little policeman saddled up the old noke he had left with us, and without saying more than *'gracias'* and *'A Dios'*, slowly trotted away, taking with him his gruesome trophy. From that day on, Senor, the piebald you brought today was called Luna, and I hope you will not change this name for any other."

Without waiting for my reply, the old gaucho rose, and bidding all of us good night, shuffled off towards a shed, moving awkwardly like an alligator walking on dry land.

So now, gentle reader, you know how I got my first horse, and why I continued to call him "Luna" which, in English, means Moon.

And with this I bid you *A Dios* and wish you happy hunting.

THE BIRTH OF A KING

MARGUERITE HENRY

from King of the Wind

IN THE NORTH-WESTERN slice of Africa known as Morocco, a horse-boy stood, with broom in hand, in the vast courtyard of the royal stables of the Sultan. He was waiting for dusk to fall.

All day long he had eaten nothing. He had not even tasted the jujubes tucked in his turban nor the enormous purple grapes that spilled over the palace wall into the stable yard. He had tried not to sniff the rich, warm fragrance of ripening pomegranates. For this was the sacred month of Ramadan when, day after day, all faithful Mohammedans neither eat nor drink from the dawn before sunrise until the moment after sunset.

The boy Agba had not minded the fast for himself. It was part of his religion. But when Signor Achmet, Chief of the Grooms, commanded that the horses, too, observe the fast, Agba's dark eyes smouldered with anger.

"It is the order of the Sultan!" the Signor had announced to the horse-boys. And he had cuffed Agba on the head when the boy showed his disapproval.

Of the twelve thousand horses in the Sultan's stables,

Agba had charge of ten. He fed and watered them and polished their coats and cleaned their stalls. Best of all, he wheeled the whole string into the courtyard at one time for their exercise.

There was one of the ten horses to whom Agba had lost his heart. She was a bay mare, as fleet as a gazelle, with eyes that studied him in whatever he did. The other nine horses he would lead out to the common water trough to drink. But for his bright bay he would fill a water cask from a pure spring beyond the palace gates. Then he would hold it while the mare sucked the water, her eyelashes brushing his fingers as she drank. For long moments after she had drunk her fill, she would gaze at him while the cool water dribbled from her muzzle onto his hands.

It was the mare that worried Agba now as he worked to fill in the time until the hour of sunset. The courtyard was already swept clean, but Agba pushed his palm-leaf broom as if he were sweeping all his thoughts into a little mound for the wind to carry away.

At last he hung his broom on an iron hook, alongside an endless row of brooms, and went to the mare. Her stall door was closed so that the fragrance of late clover would not drift in to prick her appetite. He found her asleep, lying on her side, her great belly distended by the little colt soon to be born. Agba noticed, with a heavy feeling in his chest, that the fast was telling on the mare. He could read it in the sunken places above each eye, in the harshness of her coat.

But soon the fast would be over. It was the last day of the month, and even now the sun was sinking below the grey-green olive trees that fringed the courtyard.

There was no sound anywhere, not from the palace walls beyond, nor from the quarters over the stables where the horse-boys lived. The whole world seemed to be holding its breath, waiting for dusk to fall. Small voices of insects and birds were beginning to pierce the quiet. Twilight toads piping on their bassoons. Crickets chirping. Wood doves cooing. And afar off in the Atlas Mountains a hyena began to laugh. These were the forerunners of the darkness. It would only be a short time now.

Agba turned towards the east, his eyes on the minaret of the mosque. It was a sharp needle pricking the blood-red reflection of the sun. He gazed fixedly at it until his eyes smarted. At last a figure in white robes emerged from the tower. It was the public crier. He was sounding his trumpet. He was crying four times to the four winds of heaven. The fast of Ramadan was at an end!

The air went wild with noise. Twelve thousand horses recognized the summons and neighed their hunger. The royal stables seethed like an anthill. Horse-boys swarmed out of the corridors and into the courtyard. From the hoods of their cloaks, from waistbands and vests, they took dates and raisins and almonds and popped them noisily into their mouths. They stripped the grapes from their vines. They ate with boisterous abandon. Some plunged their faces into the troughs and sucked the water as if they were horses.

Agba did not join the other horse-boys. He returned to the mare. Moving slowly so as not to frighten her, he reached under the saddle hung on the wall and found the water vessel he had filled and hidden there an hour ago. He poured the water into a basin and waited for the mare to awaken.

As if she had heard in her dreams the sound made by the water, she woke with a jerk and struggled to her feet. She came to Agba and drank. Then she raised her head, letting the water slobber from her lips.

Agba waited motionless, knowing she would want more and more. Her deep brown eyes studied him as if to say, "You are the source of all that his good."

A great happiness welled up inside Agba. He nodded, seeming to understand her thoughts, then waited while she drank again and again.

When Agba came out of the mare's stall, the other boys were beginning to lead their horses to the common trough to drink. He must hurry now if he hoped to get his corn ration first. He picked up a bag made of hemp and ran though a maze of corridors and down a steep staircase to the underground granary. At the entrance stood Signor Achmet, Chief of the Grooms. Signor Achmet was dark and bearded. In his right hand he carried a knotted stick, and from the sash at his waist hung a hundred keys. When he saw Agba, he gripped the boy's shoulder with fingers as strong as the claws of an eagle.

"Why do you not eat with the other slave-boys?" he asked in his cracked voice. Then with a sharp look he released Agba and began peeling an orange with his fingernails. His beady eyes did not leave Agba's face as he ate the orange, making loud sucking noises to show how juicy and good it was.

Agba gulped. He studied his brown toes.

"Is it the mare?"

The boy's eyes flew to the Signor's.

"Is tonight her hour?"

Slowly, gravely, Agba nodded.

"Tonight then," the Signor said, as he wiped his mouth on his mantle and began fumbling for the key to the granary, "tonight you will not go to your quarters to sleep. You will move the mare into the brood-mare stable. You will remain on watch and call me when she is ready to foal. The all-seeing eye of Allah will be upon you."

Agba's heart fluttered like bird wings. The Chief of Grooms was letting him stay with his mare! He forgot all the cuffs and sharp words. He bowed low, impatient to hear the sound of the key turning the great lock, impatient for the creaking of the door and the mingled odours of corn and barley.

The key scraped. The door creaked open. The warm, mellow smells leaked out.

Signor Achmet stood aside. Agba slipped past him into the darkness. Quickly his sensitive fingers sought the good, sound ears of corn. He filled his bag with them. Then he turned and fled up the stairs.

But the mare would not eat the corn Agba brought. She only lipped it, then closed her eyes with a great weariness.

Agba was troubled as he watered and fed the other horses in his aisle, as he ate his own meal of barley and goat's milk, as he hurried to the brood-mare stable.

Signor Achmet must have been there before him. One of the stalls was wide open, and a lantern hung on a peg, sending out a feeble light. The stall had not been used since spring and had a fusty smell. Agba leaped upon the manger and threw open a tiny round window. It showed a patch of sky and the new moon.

"This is a favourable sign," he thought. "A new moon. A new month. The foal will be strong and swift." He took a deep breath of the cool summer night. Then quickly he went to work, filling bucket after bucket of sand from the huge sand pile behind the stables. Back and forth he ran, dumping the sand on the floor of the stall. Next he covered it with straw, spreading it out first with his hands, then trotting over it, galloping over it, around and around. At last he surveyed his work with approval. It would be a good bed for the mare!

Just as he was filling the manger with fodder, Signor Achmet, in flowing white robes, looked in. He tested the depth of the sand with a bony forefinger. He felt the straw.

"You waste the sand and the straw," he said with a black look. "Half would do." But the Signor understood Agba's concern for the mare. "Fetch her now," he commanded.

Agba's bow was lost in the darkness.

"And you will summon me when she grows restless."

Swiftly and silently the Signor turned upon his heel, his white mantle fluttering behind him like moth wings.

The new moon hung over Agba's shoulder as he ran to get the mare. She was standing patiently in a corner of her stall, her head lowered, her tail tucked in. Placing a hand on her neck, Agba led her out into the night, past endless stalls and under endless archways to her new quarters. She walked slowly, heavily.

At the door of the new stall a tremor of fear shook her. She made a feeble attempt to go back, but Agba held her firmly, humming to hide his own nameless fears.

She entered the stall. She tried the soft bed with her feet. She went to the manger. Her nostrils widened to snuff the dried grasses, but she did not eat. She put her lips to the water cask but did not drink. At last she tucked her hooves underneath her and with a groan lay down. Her head nodded. She steadied it in the straw. Then her breathing, too, steadied.

As Agba stood on watch, his mind was a mill wheel, turning, turning, turning. He trembled, remembering the time he and the mare had come upon a gazelle, and he had ridden the mare alongside the gazelle, and she had outrun the wild thing. Agba could still feel the wind singing in his ears.

By closing his eyes he brought back the whole day. On the way home they had passed a wizened old storyteller in the streets, who, when Agba came near, motioned him close. The old man placed his hand on the mare's head. Then, in a voice that was no more than a whisper, he had said, "When Allah created the horse, he said to the wind, 'I will that a creature proceed from thee. Condense thyself.' And the wind condensed itself, and the result was the horse."

The words danced in Agba's head as he watched the sleeping mare. I will that a creature proceed from thee.

Condense thyself! I will that a creature proceed from thee. Condense thyself! He told the words over and over in his mind until suddenly the stable walls faded away and Agba was riding the South Wind. And there was nothing to stop him. No palace walls. No trees. Nor hedges. Nor rivers. Only white clouds to ride through, and a blue vaulted archway, and the wind for a mount.

With a sigh he sank down in the straw. His head dropped.

The boy's dreams spun themselves out until there was nothing left of them. He slept a deep sleep. The candle in the lantern sputtered and died. The new moon rode higher and higher. Bats and nighthawks, flying noiselessly in the velvet night, went about their business, swooping insects out of the air. With the grey light of morning they vanished, giving way to the jangling chorus of the crows.

Agba woke. The stable walls had closed in again. And there was the mare lying on her side as before. But her head was raised now, and she was drying off a newborn foal! Her tongue-strokes filled the silence of the stall, licking, licking, licking.

The boy watched in fear that if he took his eyes away the whole scene might vanish into the mist of the morning. Oh, how tiny the foal was! And so wet there was no telling what its colour would be. But its eyes were open. And they were full of curiosity.

Agba's body quivered with the wonder of the little fellow's birth. He had seen newborn foals before, but none so small and finely made. In the distance he could her the softly padding feet of the horse-boys. He could hear the wild boar grunting and coughing in his hole behind the stables. He wondered if the boar really did keep evil spirits from entering into the horses.

Afraid to move, he watched the mare clumsily get to her feet. He watched her nudge the young thing with her nose.

The foal tried to get up. He thrust out his forefeet, but

they splayed and he seemed to get all tangled up with himself. He tried again and again. For one breathless instant he was on his feet. Then his legs buckled and he fell in a little heap. Agba reached a hand toward him, but the mare came between. She pushed the little one with her nose. She pushed him with her tongue. She nickered to him. He was trying again. He was standing up. How spindly he was! And his ribs showed. And he had hollows above his eyes just like his dam.

"I could carry him in my arms," thought Agba. "He is not much bigger than a goat, and he has long whiskers like a goat. Long and silky. And his tail is curly. And he is all of one colour. Except – except . . ." Suddenly the boy's heart missed a beat. On the off hind heel there was a white spot. It was no bigger than an almond, but it was there! The white spot – the emblem of swiftness!

Agba leaped to his feet. He wanted to climb the tower of the mosque. He wanted to blow on the trumpet. He wanted to cry to the four winds of heaven: "A foal is born. And he will be swift as the wind of the desert, for on his hind heel is a white spot. A white spot. A white . . ."

Just then a shaft of early sunlight pierced the window of the stable and found the colt. It flamed his coat into red gold. It made a sun halo around his head.

Agba was full of fear. He opened his mouth, but no sound escaped. Maybe this was all a dream. Maybe the foal was not real. The golden coat. The crown of sun rays. Maybe he was a golden horse belonging to the chariot of the sun!

"I'll capture him with a name," the boy thought quickly. And he named the young thing Sham, which is the Arabic word for sun.

No sooner had Agba fastened a name on him than the little creature seemed to take on a new strength. He took a few steps. He found his mother's milk. He began to nurse, making soft, sucking noises.

Agba knew he should be reporting to Signor Achmet. He knew he should be standing in line for his measure of corn. But he could not bear to break the spell. He listened to the colt suckling, to the mare munching the dried grasses. He smelled their warm bodies. A stable was a good place to be born.

THE SENTINEL

WALTER FARLEY

from The Black Stallion Revolts

THE GREY GELDING, Napoleon, was built from the ground up and butter fat. His roundness was not due to overfeeding or lack of exercise but to a most placid disposition and an ease of adapting himself to any kind of situation or way of life. He stood with one hind foot drawn in an easy, relaxed position and eyes half-closed. Only his long ears moved, and they just wobbled as if the weight of them was too much for him to bear at this particular moment. He was the picture of contentment; as peaceful as the June night which enveloped him. There was no reason for him to appear otherwise. He was most happy with his life. He was no youngster.

The grass of his paddock moved in the night breeze, giving it the soft, liquid motion of the sea. There were stars and a moon, and together they shone frostlike on the fences and roofs of the barns and main house a short distance away.

Finally the old grey roused himself to saunter about his paddock. His movements were slow and quiet. He was very particular in his choice of grass. He would stop only long enough to crop a few mouthfuls, then go on to other grasses that appealed more to his fancy and discriminating taste. But it wasn't long before he returned to his favourite haunt beneath the billowing oak tree. He closed his eyes again.

All was quiet, and as it should be. The inky silhouette of a tall, black stallion moved in the adjacent paddock to his left. Teeth clicked sharply as the stallion cut the grass low and even.

The grey's wobbling ears were keen, and by using them he followed the movements of the Black. He was well aware, too, of the whereabouts of the burly, black horse in still another paddock, the one on his right. He had heard Satan snort a few moments ago.

The breeze became stronger, gently whipping his body with a shower of deep evening coolness. After the heat of the day it felt very good. That there were no flies to bother him added to his enjoyment. For ideal comfort this was the way it should be. A fly-protected barn during the day, and at night the freedom of the paddocks. For several weeks now the horses had been allowed this privilege. It would continue as long as there was peace in the paddocks. All this the old grey knew very well; his vast experience told him so.

He knew why he occupied the paddock between the Black and Satan. To keep his head, to think for himself, to do what was expected of him . . . these things he had learned long ago. He did his duties willingly, whether he was on the track, helping to school young and eager yearlings in their first lessons, or here in the paddock, where he was ever watchful of the actions of mature stallions. Knowing that he was wanted, that he had a job to do, gave him a warm consciousness of virtue and well-being. He opened his eyes, took in the paddock fences, and then, as though receiving comfort and security from their great height, permitted his eyelids to drop again. This time he went fast asleep.

He awakened to the sound of a strong wind. The skies had turned black. The moon was blanketed by heavy, running clouds and the stars were mere pinpoints in the heavens, shedding no light below. The oak tree afforded the grey horse protection against the wind and he was loath to leave it. Besides, there was no reason for him to go. He need only stay here and wait out the wind. If it got worse and became a storm, he was certain that soon he would see the lights go on in the house, and shortly thereafter he and the others would be taken into their stalls. He moved closer to the great trunk of the tree, and for a while just listened to the racing winds above him.

It was the wind and the blackness of the night that diverted Napoleon's attention from the movements of the tall stallion in the next paddock. For a long while he had trotted lightly and warily along the fence, only his eyes disclosing the excitement that burned within him. He made no sound except for the slight, hushed beat of his hoofs over the grass. He did not shrill his challenge to the burly stallion two paddocks away from him. It was not yet time. The Black was clever and able to control the savage instinct that sought release within his great body.

The wind whipped his mane, and his tail, set high, billowed behind him. He stopped again to measure the height of the fence. In spite of his long limbs he had stretch his head to touch the top board. He moved on to the front corner of the paddock, facing the barn. Once more he tested his strength against the centre boards at this particular spot. They bent as they had before. He pushed harder this time. They cracked and split. He stopped using his strength, waiting almost cunningly until deciding on his next move. The fire in his eyes was mounting.

Carefully he lowered himself to the ground, pressing the weight of his body against the bottom board. Then he rolled away and struck a smashing blow against it with his hind feet. It split as had the others. Still on his back, he rolled back and forth, using his great body like a pendulum against the boards. But he did not ram his weight like a blundering bruiser. Instead, with cunning and skill he manoeuvred his body, using pressure against the split boards only when he knew they were most apt to give completely. Finally they broke and were swept outward as he rolled under the top board. The Black was free of his confining paddock!

He got to his feet with the speed and agility of the wildest and most savage of animals. A striking change had swept over his glistening body. No longer was he calm and cunning, but trembling and brutally eager to kill. Gone was his domesticity and the inner control that had kept the fire from his eyes and given the coolness to his blood. Now he was inflamed with a terrible but natural instinct to do battle with another stallion. He turned his gleaming, red eyes on Satan, two paddocks beyond; then he hurled forth his screaming challenge, and its shrillness rose above the cry of the wind.

He was already on his way down the dirt road fronting the paddocks when the grey gelding came plunging to the fence. The stallion paid not the slightest attention to him. The grey ran with his ears back, his teeth snapping in rage between the boards because he knew the stallion's savage intent, and could do nothing to keep him from the black horse beyond. The gelding stopped when he came to the end of his enclosure. He neighed loudly and incessantly, knowing this was the only useful thing he could do. But his warnings of the disturbed peace were deadened by the force of the wind. The main house remained dark.

Turning from the dirt road, the tall stallion ran down the corridor between the paddocks. Every possible precaution had been taken to make the paddocks foolproof, to keep one stallion from another, to forestall just such an emergency as this. The paddock fences were strong and high, the corridor wide. Yet the Black was loose, and in spite of the fence still separating him from Satan, his fury was not to be denied. He ran with reckless speed down the corridor and back again, once hurling himself against the fence only to be repelled. He ignored the grey gelding, who followed his every move still neighing in rage. He had eyes only for the large, black horse who stood so quietly in the centre of his paddock. That Satan did not move, that he uttered no scream accepting the challenge, infuriated the tall stallion even more. His nostrils were distended in

112

recognition of the hateful scent of his rival as he finally left the corridor and approached Satan's paddock from the front.

He went to the fence screaming. Lifting his head, he touched his nose to the top board. Then he rose on hind legs to bring his forehoofs down upon it. He was terrible in his fury, but his act proved futile. Frenzied rage had replaced the cool cunningness of his earlier behaviour. He rose again, trying to batter down the fence, and his legs hurt from the crashing impact of his blows. The fence remained intact. He whirled while still at his utmost height, his hind legs pivoting his great body with uncanny grace and swiftness, then sending him away from the fence in long strides. It was less than a hundred feet to the barn, and there he stopped short with tossing head and mane. With no hesitation he whirled again and swept back, his strides lengthening with startling swiftness for so short a distance. He gathered his great body in front of the fence as though to jump it, but he never unleashed his spring. Instead he stopped short again, stomping the earth with both forefeet in his frenzy and frustration.

He turned to the left to run along the fence. He had passed the paddock gate when suddenly he felt the earth rise gradually beneath his running hoofs, and then descend abruptly. He went on for a short distance before stopping and going back to the elevated stretch of ground which was used in the loading and unloading of horses from vans. Now he was more quiet, more cunning. He walked up the gradual ascent to the flat summit of the grassy mound. For a moment he stood there, his wild eyes seeming to measure the distance to the fence. His added height enabled him to see over the top board, and he screamed again at the horse beyond. There was a new note to his whistle, for now he knew the battle was close at hand. Satan, too, was aware of it; he screamed for the first time . . . and his answer was as shrill, as terrible in its savageness as his challenger's.

The Black turned, leaving the mound, and went once

more as far as the barn. He whirled and bolted, picking up speed with every stride. He gathered himself going up the grassy incline. At the top he rose in the air, hurling himself forward, his legs tucked well beneath him. A hoof struck the top of the fence but did not upset him. He came down, and without breaking stride raced forward to meet Satan.

He went only a short distance before he came to a plunging stop, the cool logic that had helped him win battles with other stallions coming to the fore. His eyes were still blazing with hate, his ears were flat against his head. But when he moved again it was to encircle his opponent with strides that were light and cautious.

Both fear and fire shone in Satan's eyes. He did not want to fight yet he stood unflinching and ready. He was heavier than if not as tall as the Black. His bones were larger, his neck shorter and more bulging with muscle, his head heavier. Yet his great, thick body had the same fascination and swiftness of movement as the stallion who encircled him. He had inherited these together with his tremendous speed from the Black, his sire. Now, keeping his bright eyes on his opponent, he began to move with him. He heard him scream again, and answered. He waited for the fight to be brought to him. He was ready.

Yet when the attack came, it was with the swiftness of light, and even though Satan had thought himself prepared he barely had time to rise and meet the horrible onslaught. Two raging furies, hateful to see, began a combat that would end only with the death of one!

The first light that went on was in the apartment over the broodmare barn, just past the main house. Seconds later a short, stocky man, wearing only pyjamas and slippers, came running out the door. He moved ghostlike in the wind, his face as white as his dishevelled hair. His bowlegs spun like a wheel as his strides came faster. He lost one loose slipper. He kicked the other off without breaking his run. Only when he came to the main house did he stop, and then just for a second. Cupping large hands around his mouth, he let loose a scream in the direction of the open window on the second floor.

"Alec! Alec! Alec!"

The wind hurled his cries aside. He didn't know if he'd been heard and he couldn't wait to find out. He started running again, his blood hammering within his chest, but not from his exertion. His eyes were dimmed and wet, but not from the wind. He had just seen the Black clear the fence into Satan's paddock. He knew what the consequences would be.

Nearing the fence, he saw the silhouette of the attacker encircling Satan. He knew he was too late, that the clash of bodies would come in seconds. His face grew even paler, yet uncontrollable rage was there, too. His body and voice trembled as he roared, "Away! Away!, you killer!" But he knew the Black didn't hear him, and that even if he did the command would have little effect.

He ran to the stallion barn and flung open the door, looking for any weapons he might use. A leather riding whip hung on a peg in the entryway. He took it. A pitchfork stood by the door. He grabbed this, too, and ran outside again. Reaching the paddock gate, he pulled it open wide, and charged towards the black bodies now wrapped in a deadly embrace.

He screamed at them, but his voice was just a muted whisper beneath the crashing blows of forehoofs that pounded in furious battle. Suddenly, from their great height, the stallions toppled and fell, their bodies shaking the very earth. The man sprang forward, trying to get between them with his pitchfork. But their action was too fast and terrifying, and his efforts were futile. They bounded to lightning feet and clashed again, their heads extended long and snakelike as they sought with bared teeth to tear and rend each other.

Unmindful of his own safety, the man moved forward with his puny weapons. As yet neither stallion had drawn blood. But in a matter of seconds, if he couldn't separate them, it would be too late. They were locked together, seemingly suspended in the air. Each sought the other's windpipe for the vicious hold that would mean certain death. The man's breath came in fast, hard gasps as he tried to thrust the pitchfork between them, to divert their attention to him. Even now he knew he could control Satan if he ever got the chance. But there would be no opportunity, not with the Black, that hellion, forcing the fight, determined on destruction!

The stallions lost their holds, and came screaming down again. The Black whirled, letting fly his hind hoofs in an awful blow which, if it had landed full, would have sent Satan reeling. But the burly horse saw the hoofs coming. He shifted his great body with amazing agility, and the crashing hind legs only grazed him. Nevertheless, although he had avoided serious injury, the glancing blow sent him off balance. He stumbled and went down.

At this moment the man plunged forward, reaching the Black before he could whirl on the fallen horse. In his fury he used the leather riding-crop, bringing it down hard again and again against the stallion's lathered hindquarters. A great tremor racked the Black's body as the blows landed. Suddenly he turned upon the man, all his savageness now directed upon him.

With pitchfork extended the man fell back. He shouted futile commands as the stallion plunged towards him and then stopped before the steel prongs of the fork. The man knew his life was in great danger, yet he stole a second to glance at Satan, who was climbing to his feet. If only Satan would go through the open gate of the paddock! If only he could keep the Black away and get out himself! He backed towards the gate shouting, "Out Satan! Out!" But the words barely left his lips before the Black came at him again, and he raised the pitchfork in his defence. He struck hard, viciously, and the stallion fell back.

The man saw Satan moving towards the gate. Then, running past the horse, came Alec! He shouted the boy's name and waited for him, without lowering his pitchfork.

Alec came to a stop. He stood still until he was certain the Black's wild eyes were on him, then he walked forward, his bare feet making no sound.

Still pale with rage and terror, the man cried, "Take the whip, Alec! Use it on him if you have to!"

Without taking his eyes off the Black, Alec said, "If I did, he'd kill me, Henry. The same as he would have killed you." He continued walking forward, talking to the stallion in a soft, low voice, and never raising it or his hand in a gesture of any kind. Only once did he interrupt his murmurings with a soft-spoken command. When he got close to the Black, he put his hand on the lathered halter. The stallion trembled, and for a moment his eyes gleamed brighter than ever. Alec gave the low command again, but the stallion drew back his head in an abrupt gesture of defiance.

Keeping his hands on the halter, Alec moved along with the stallion until he came to a stop. The boy waited patiently, his eyes never leaving those of his horse, his murmurings never ceasing. With a motion of his head, he indicated to Henry that he was to leave.

Alec turned the Black towards the upper end of the paddock, diverting his attention from Satan and Henry. With his free hand he tried to soothe the tossing head, and finally he got the stallion to take a few steps up the paddock. Then the Black stopped again, trying to turn his head.

Alec held him close, and waited for a while before leading him forward once more. Satan and Henry had left the paddock. It was a little easier now. The Black followed Alec for a moment before stopping again, this time to utter his short, piercing blast. Alec stood quietly beside him, the wind billowing his pyjamas. He knew that in a little while the Black would calm down, and he would be able to take him into the barn. But right now he must go on as he was doing, talking to him, soothing him, and waiting.

He walked him again, and as he did, he tried to understand the reason for the Black's sudden, vicious attack on Satan. For many months his horse had been all a well-mannered stallion should be. Why, then, had he reverted to the role of a killer tonight? And what were he and Henry going to do about it?

THE HORSE FAIR

DAPHNE DU MAURIER

from Jamaica Inn

Mary has escaped for the day from the sinister goings-on at Jamaica Inn where she lives with her uncle and aunt, and is visiting Launceston Christmas fair with Jem, who is a horse thief but also a good and faithful friend.

THIS WAS A gay and happy world to Mary. The town was set on the bosom of a hill, with a castle framed in the centre, like a tale from old history. There were trees clustered here, and sloping fields, and water gleamed in the valley below. The moors were remote; they stretched away out of sight behind the town, and were forgotten. Launceston had reality; those people were alive. Christmas came into its own again in the town and had a place amongst the cobbled streets, the laughing jostling crowd, and the watery sun struggled from his hiding-place behind the grey-banked clouds to join the festivity. Mary wore the handkerchief Jem had given her. She even unbent so far as to permit him to tie the ends under her chin. They had stabled the pony and jingle at the tip of the town, and now Jem pushed his way through the crowd, leading his two stolen horses, Mary following at his heels. He led the way with confidence, making straight for the main square, where the whole of Launceston gathered, and the booths and tents of the Christmas fair stood end to end. There was a place roped off from the fair for the buying and selling of livestock, and the ring was surrounded by farmers and countrymen, gentlemen too, and dealers from Devon and beyond. Mary's heart beat faster as they approached the ring; supposing there was someone from North Hill here, or a farmer from a neighbouring village, surely they would recognize the horses? Jem wore his hat at the back of his head, and he whistled. He looked back at her once and winked his eye. The crowd parted and made way for him. Mary stood on the outskirts, behind a fat market-woman with a basket, and she saw Jem take his place amongst a group of men with ponies, bending as he did so to a flare to light his pipe. He looked cool and unperturbed. Presently a flashy-looking fellow with a square hat and cream breeches thrust his way through the crowd and crossed over to the horses. His voice was loud and important, and he kept hitting his boot with a crop, and then pointing to the ponies. From his tone, and his air of authority Mary judged him to be a dealer. Soon he was joined by a little lynx-eyed man in a black coat, who now and again jogged his elbow and whispered in his ear.

Mary saw him stare hard at the black pony that had belonged to Squire Bassat; he went up to him, and bent down and felt his legs. Then he whispered something in the ear of the loud-voiced man. Mary watched him nervously.

"Where did you get this pony?" said the dealer, tapping Jem on the shoulder. "He was never bred on the moors, not with that head and shoulders."

"He was foaled at Callington four years ago," said Jem carelessly, his pipe in the corner of his mouth. "I bought him as a yearling from old Tim Bray; you remember Tim? He sold up last year and went into Dorset. Tim always told me I'd get my money back on this pony. The dam was Irish bred, and won prizes up-country. Have a look at him, won't you? But he's not going cheap, I'll tell you that."

He puffed at his pipe, while the two men went over the pony carefully. The time seemed endless before they straightened themselves and stood back. "Had any trouble with his skin?" said the lynx-eyed man. "It feels very coarse on the surface, and sharp like bristles. There's a taint about him, too, I don't like. You haven't been doping him have you?"

"There's nothing ailing with that pony," replied Jem. "The other one, there, he fell away to nothing in the summer, but I've brought him back all right. I'd do better to keep him till the spring now, I believe, but he's costing me money. No, this black pony here, you can't fault him. I'll be frank with you over one thing, and it's only fair to

admit it. Old Tim Bray never knew the mare was in foal – he was in Plymouth at the time, and his boy was looking after her – and when he found out he gave the boy a thrashing, but of course it was too late. He had to make the best of a bad job. It's my opinion the sire was grey; look at the short grey hair there, close to the skin – that's grey, isn't it? Tim just missed a good bargain with this pony. Look at those shoulders; there's breeding for you. I tell you what, I'll take eighteen guineas for him." The lynx-eyed man shook his head, but the dealer hesitated.

"Make it fifteen and we might do business," he suggested.

"No, eighteen guineas is my sum, and not a penny less," said Jem.

The two men consulted together and appeared to disagree. Mary heard the word 'fake', and Jem shot a glance at her over the heads of the crowd. A little murmur rose from the group of men beside him. Once more the lynx-eyed man bent and touched the legs of the black pony. "I'd advise another opinion on this pony," he said. "I'm not satisfied about him myself. Where's your mark?"

Jem showed him the narrow slit in the ear and the man examined it closely.

"You're a sharp customer, aren't you?" said Jem. "Anyone would think I'd stolen the horse. Anything wrong with the mark?"

"No, apparently not. But it's a good thing for you that Tim Bray has gone to Dorset. He'd never own this pony, whatever you like to say. I wouldn't touch him, Stevens, if I were you. You'll find yourself in trouble. Come away, man."

The loud-voiced dealer looked regretfully at the black pony.

"He's a good-looker," he said. "I don't care who bred him, or if his sire was piebald. What makes you so particular, Will?"

Once more the lynx-eyed man plucked at his sleeve and

whispered in his ear. The dealer listened, and pulled a face, and then he nodded. "All right," he said aloud; "I've no doubt that you're right. You've got an eye for trouble, haven't you? Perhaps we're better out of it. You can keep your pony," he added to Jem. "My partner doesn't fancy him. Take my advice and come down on your price. If you have him for long on your hands you'll be sorry." And he elbowed his way through the crowd with the lynx-eyed man beside him, and they disappeared in the direction of the White Hart. Mary breathed a sigh of relief when she saw the last of them. She could make nothing of Jem's expression; his lips were framed in the inevitable whistle. People came and went; the shaggy moorland ponies were sold for two or three pounds apiece, and their late owners departed satisfied. No one came near the black pony again. He was looked at askance by the crowd. At a quarter to four Jem sold the other horse for six pounds to a cheerful, honest-looking farmer, after a long and very good-humoured argument. The farmer declared he would give five pounds, and Jem stuck out for seven. After twenty minutes' riotous bargaining the sum of six pounds was agreed, and the farmer rode off on the back of his purchase with a grin from ear to ear. Mary began to flag on her feet. Twilight gathered in the market square and the lamps were lit. The town wore an air of mystery. She was thinking of returning to the jingle when she heard a woman's voice behind her, and a high affected laugh. She turned and saw a woman dressed in a blue cloak and a plumed hat. "Oh, look, James," she was saying. "Did you ever see such a delicious pony in your life? He holds his head just like poor Beauty did. The likeness would be quite striking, only this animal of course is black, and has nothing of Beauty's breeding. What a nuisance Roger isn't here. I can't disturb him from his meeting. What do you think of him, James?"

Her companion put up his eyeglass and stared. "Damn it, Maria," he drawled, "I don't know a thing about horses. The pony you lost was a grey wasn't it? This thing is ebony, positively ebony, my dear. Do you want to buy him?"

The woman gave a little trill of laughter. "It would be such a good Christmas present for the children," she said. "They've plagued poor Roger ever since Beauty disappeared. Ask the price, James, will you?"

The man strutted forward. "Here, my good fellow," he called to Jem, "do you want to sell that black pony of yours?"

Jem shook his head. "He's promised to a friend," he said. "I wouldn't like to go back on my word. Besides, this pony wouldn't carry you. He's been ridden by children."

"Oh, really. Oh, I see. Oh, thank you. Maria, this fellow says the pony is not for sale."

"Is he sure? What a shame. I'd set my heart on him. I'll pay him his price tell him. Ask him again, James."

Once more the man put up his glass and drawled, "Look here, my man, this lady has taken a fancy to your pony. She has just lost one, and she wants to replace him. Her children will be most disappointed if they hear about it. Damn your friend, you know. He must wait. What is your price?"

"Twenty-five guineas," said Jem promptly. "At least, that's what my friend was going to pay. I'm not anxious to sell him."

The lady in the plumed hat swept into the ring. "I'll give you thirty for him." she said. "I'm Mrs Bassat from North Hill, and I want the pony as a Christmas present for my children. Please don't be obstinate. I have half the sum here in my purse, and this gentleman will give you the rest. Mr Bassat is in Launceston now and I want the pony to be a surprise to him as well as to my children. My groom shall fetch the pony immediately, and ride him to North Hill before Mr Bassat leaves the town. Here's the money."

Jem swept off his hat and bowed low. "Thank you, madam," he said. "I hope Mr Bassat will be pleased with your bargain. You will find the pony exceedingly safe with children."

"Oh, I'm certain he will be delighted. Of course the pony is nothing like the one we had stolen. Beauty was a thoroughbred, and worth a great deal of money. This little animal is handsome enough, and will please the children. Come along, James; it's getting quite dark, and I'm chilled to the bone."

She made her way from the ring towards the coach that waited in the square. The tall footman leapt forward to open the door. "I've just bought a pony for Master Robert and Master Henry," she said. "Will you find Richards and tell him he's to ride it back home? I want it to be a surprise to the squire." She stepped into the coach, her petticoats fluttering behind her, followed by her companion with the monocle.

Jem looked hastily over his shoulder, and tapped a lad who stood behind him on the arm. "Here," he said, "would you like a five-shilling piece?" The lad nodded, his mouth agape. "Hang on to this will you? I've just had word that my wife has given birth to twins and her life is in danger. I haven't a moment to lose. Here, take the bridle. A happy Christmas to you."

And he was off in a moment, walking hard across the square, his hands thrust deep in his breeches pocket. Mary followed, a discreet ten paces behind. Her face was scarlet and she kept her eyes on the ground. The laughter bubbled up inside her and she hid her mouth in her shawl. She was near to collapsing when they reached the farther side of the square, out of sight of the coach and the group of people, and she stood with her hand to her side catching her breath. Jem waited for her, his face as grave as a judge.

"Jem Merlyn, you deserve to be hanged," she said, when she had recovered herself. "To stand there as you did in the market square and sell that stolen pony back to Mrs Bassat herself! You have the cheek of the Devil, and the hairs on my head have gone grey from watching you."

He threw back his head and laughed, and she could not resist him. Their laughter echoed in the street until people turned to look at them, and they too caught the infection, and smiled, and broke into laughter; and Launceston itself seemed to rock in merriment as peal after peal of gaiety echoed in the street, mingling with the bustle and clatter of the fair; and with it all there was shouting, and calling, and a song from somewhere. The torches and the flares cast strange lights on the faces of people, and there was colour, and shadow, and the hum of voices, and a ripple of excitement in the air.

THE OUTLAW

SINCLAIR ROSS

S HE WAS BEAUTIFUL but dangerous. She had thrown one
man and killed him, thrown another and broken his
collar bone, and my parents, as if they knew what
the sight of her idle in her stall was doing to me, never let a
day go by without giving lurid details, everything from
splints and stitches to the undertaker, of the painful and
untimely end in store for me should I ever take it into my
fool young head to try to ride her.

"I've got troubles enough without having you laid up
with broken bones and doctor's bills. She's a sly one, mind,
and no good's ever come of her."

"Besides, you're only turned thirteen, and a grown man,
a regular cowboy at that, would think twice before tackling
her. Another year and then we'll see. You'll both be that
much older. In the meantime nobody expects it of you."

In the meantime, though, she was a captive, pining her
heart away. Week after week she stamped and pawed,
nosed the hay out of her manger contemptuously, flung up
her head and poured out wild, despairing neighs into the
prairie winds and blizzards streaming past. It was mostly,

128

of course, for my benefit. She had sized me up, evidently, as soft-hearted as well as faint-hearted, and decided there was just a chance that I might weaken and go riding. Her neighs, just as she intended they should, tormented and shamed me.

She was a good horse, but a reprobate. That was how we came to own her. At the auction sale where she was put up, her reputation as a killer spread among the crowd, and my father got her cheap. He was such a practical, level-headed man, and she was so obviously a poor investment, that I suspect it was because of me he bought her. As I stood at his side in the front row of the crowd and watched them lead her out, poised, dramatic, radiant, some of the sudden desire that overwhelmed me must have leaped from my face and melted him.

"Anyway, she's a bargain," he defended himself that evening at the supper table. "I can always sell her and at least get back what I paid. But first I want to see what a taste of good hard work will do."

He tried it. His intention was to work her on the land a month or two, just till she was tamed down to make an all-round, serviceable saddle horse, but after a painful week of half-days on the plough he let her keep her stall. She was too hard on his nerves, he said, straining ahead and pulling twice her share. She was too hard on his self-respect, actually, the slender limbs, the imperious head.

For she was a very lovely reprobate. Twenty years of struggle with the land had made him a determined, often hard man, but he couldn't bring himself to break her spirit with the plough.

She was one horse, and she was all horses. Thundering battle chargers, fleet Arabians, untamed mustangs – sitting beside her on her manger I knew and rode them all. There was history in her shapely head and burning eyes. I charged with her at Balaklava, Waterloo, scoured the deserts of Africa and the steppes of the Ukraine. Conquest and carnage, trumpets and glory – she understood, and carried me triumphantly.

To approach her was to be enlarged, transported. She was coal-black, gleaming, queenly. Her mane had a ripple and her neck an arch. And somehow, softly and mysteriously, she was always burning. The reflection on her glossy hide, whether of winter sunshine or yellow lantern light, seemed the glow of some fierce, secret passion. There were moments when I felt the whole stable charged with her, as if she were the priestess of her kind, in communion with her deity.

For all that, though, she was a very dangerous horse, and dutifully my parents kept warning me. Facts didn't lie, they pointed out. A record was a record.

Isabel did her utmost to convince me that the record was a slander. With nuzzling, velvet lips she coaxed and pleaded, whispered that the delights of fantasy and dream were but as shadows beside the exhilarations of reality. Only try reality – slip her bridle on. Only be reasonable – ask myself what she would gain by throwing me. After all, I was turned thirteen. It wasn't as if I were a small boy.

And then, temptress, she bore me off to the mountain top of my vanity, and with all the world spread out before my gaze, talked guilefully of prestige and acclaim.

Over there, three miles away, was the school house. What a sensation to come galloping up on her, the notorious outlaw, instead of jogging along as usual on bandy-legged old Pete. What a surprise for Millie Dickson, whose efforts to be loyal to me were always defeated by my lack of verve and daring. For it was true: on the playground I had only a fair rating. I was butterfingers when it came to ball, and once in a fight I had cravenly turned tail and run. How sweet to wipe out all the ignominy of my past, to be deferred to by the other boys, to bask in Millie's smiles of favour.

And over there, seven miles away, the cupolas of its grain elevators just visible on the horizon, was town. Where fairs were sometimes held, and races run. On such a horse I naturally would win, and for all I knew the prize might be a hundred dollars. Well, then – supposing I could treat Millie to ice-cream and a movie!

Here Isabel would pause a moment, contemptuous of one so craven, then let out a shrill whinny in challenge to some other rider, with heart and spirit equal to her own. There was no one, of course, to hear the challenge, but still it always troubled me. Johnny Olsen, for instance, the show-off Swede who had punched my nose and made me run – supposing he should come along and say, "I'll ride her for you – I'm not scared!" What kind of figure then would I cut? What would Millie Dickson say?

Isabel's motives, in all this, were two. The first was a natural, purely equine desire to escape from her stall and stretch her legs. The second, equally strong, was a perverse, purely feminine itch to bend me to her will.

For it was a will as imperious as her head. Her pride was at stake; I had to be reduced. With the first coaxing nuzzle of her lips she had committed herself to the struggle, and that as a male I was still at such a rudimentary stage made it doubly imperative that she emerge the victor. Defeat by a man would have been defeat, bitter but endurable. Defeat by a boy, on the other hand, would have been sheer humiliation.

On account of the roads and weather school was closed for two months after Christmas, and as the winter wore on it became increasingly difficult to resist her. A good deal of the time my father was away with wheat to town, and it was three miles to the nearest neighbour where there was another boy. I had chores, books, and the toolshop to keep me busy, but still there were long hours of idleness. Hungry for companionship, it was only natural that I should turn to Isabel. There were always her tail and mane to comb out when we wearied of each other conversationally.

My association with her, of course, was virtual disobedience. I knew that she was charging me with desire,

that eventually under its pressure I must burst like a
blister, but still, despite conscience and good intentions, I
lingered. Leaving her was always difficult, like leaving a
fair or picnic, and going home to hunt the cows.

And then one clear sharp day, early in February, Millie
Dickson and her mother drove over to spend the afternoon,
and suddenly the temptation was too much for me.

They came early, country-fashion, so that Mrs Dickson
would have time for a long talk and tea, and be home again
before nightfall. My father was away to town, and when
they drove up in their bright red cutter I hurried out to take
the horse. Mrs Dickson was generous in her thanks, and
even Millie smiled invitingly from beneath her frosted
yellow curls. She had always liked me well enough. It was
just that my behaviour at school made it difficult to be my
champion.

I was shy when I returned to the house, but exceedingly happy. We all sat in the kitchen, not only because it was the largest, warmest room, but also because it gave my mother a chance to entertain her guests and at the same time whip up fresh biscuits and a cake in their honour. Mrs Dickson asked so many friendly questions that I squirmed with pleasure till the varnish on my chair was fairly blistered. What could it mean but that at home Millie did champion me, that she suppressed the discreditable and spoke only of the best?

She and I talked, too. We leafed through old magazines, gossiped about school, speculated on the new teacher, and gradually established a sense of intimacy and good will that made me confident my past was all forgotten, my future rosy and secure. For an hour it was like that – socially the most gratifying hour I had ever spent – and then, as nearly always happened when my mother had visitors, the delinquencies and scandals of the community moved in, and the kitchen became a place unfit for innocent young ears.

There must have been a considerable number of these delinquencies. It was indeed a very upright, fine community, but it must have had its wayward side. Anyway, surveying my entire boyhood, I am sure I could count on the fingers of one hand the times I was not sent out to chop wood or look for eggs when my mother and her friends got started on the neighbours. Usually I had a fair idea from the thread of the conversation who it was who had been up to what, but this time, absorbed in my relationship with Millie, I heard nothing till my mother tapped my shoulder.

"Come along," she said brightly, affecting concern for our appetites and health. "It's too fine a day for you and Millie to be sitting in the house. Run out and play in the fresh air, so you'll be ready for your tea."

But at thirteen you don't play with a girl. You can neither skin the cat with her up in the loft among the rafters, nor turn somersaults down a strawstack. I did suggest taking the .22 and going after rabbits, but the dear little bunnies were so sweet, she said, she couldn't bear to hurt them. Naturally, therefore, after a chilly and dispiriting turn or two around the barnyard, I took her in to visit Isabel.

Isabel rose to the occasion. She minced and pawed, strained at her halter shank to let us see how badly she wanted to be taken out, then nipped our sleeves to prove her gentle playfulness. And finally, to remind us that despite such intimacies she was by no means an ordinary horse, she lifted her head and trumpeted out one of her wild, dramatic neighs.

Millie was impressed. "The wonderful way she holds her head," she said, "just like a picture. If only you could ride her to school."

"Nobody rides her – anywhere," I replied curtly. "She's an outlaw." And then, as her mouth drooped in disappointment, "At least nobody's supposed to ride her."

She jumped for it. "You mean you do ride her? And she doesn't throw you?"

"Of course," I conceded modestly, "she's very easy to ride. Such speed – and smooth as a rocking chair. When you look down the ground's just like water running past. But she could throw me all right if she had a mind to."

Millie sighed. "I'd like so much though to see you ride her. Today – isn't it a good chance, with them in there talking and your father away to town?"

I hesitated, overcome by a feeling of fright and commitment, and then Isabel too joined in. She begged and wheedled, looked so innocent, at the same time so hurt and disappointed, that Millie exclaimed she felt like going for a ride herself. And that settled it. "Stand at the door and see no one's coming," I commanded. "I'll put her bridle on."

Isabel practically put it on herself. She gave a shrill, excited whinny as I led her out, pranced like a circus pony, pushed me along still faster with her nose. "No," I answered Millie shortly, "I don't use the saddle. You don't

134

get sore, she rides so easy. And in case she turns mean I won't get tangled in the stirrups."

With a flutter in her voice Millie said, "Do you really think you should?" and in response I steeled myself, nonchalantly turned up the collar of my sheepskin. "At the rate she goes," I explained, "the wind cuts through you like a knife."

To myself I reflected, "There's plenty of snow. At the worst it will only be a spill."

Isabel stood quite still till I was mounted. She even stood still a moment longer, letting me gather myself, take a firm grip of the reins, crouch low in readiness. Then with a plunge, a spasm of muscles, she was off. And it was true: the wind cut sharp and bitter like a knife, the snow slipped past like water. Only in her motion there was a difference. She was like a rocket, not a rocking chair.

It was nearly a mile, though, before I began properly to understand what was happening. Isabel the outlaw – the horse that had killed a man, that people talked about for fifty miles – here was I just turned thirteen and riding her.

And an immense pride filled me. Cold as I was I pushed my sheepskin collar down and straightened recklessly to feel the rush of wind. I needed it that way, a counteracting sting of cold to steady the exhilaration.

We had gone another mile before I remembered Millie, and at once, as if sensitive to my concern, Isabel drew up short for breath. She didn't drop to a trot or walk as an ordinary horse would have done, but instead with the clean grace and precision of a bird alighting on a branch, came smoothly to a halt. And for a moment or two, before starting home again, she rested. The prairie spread before us cold and sparkling in the winter sunlight, and poised and motionless, ears pricked forwards, nostrils faintly quivering, she breathed in rapturously its loping miles of freedom.

And I too, responsive to her bidding, was aware as never before of its austere, unrelenting beauty. There were the white fields and the blue, metallic sky; the little splashes here and there of yellow strawstack, luminous and clear as drops of gum on fresh pine lumber; the scattered farmsteads brave and wistful in their isolation; the gleam of sun and snow. I wanted none of it, but she insisted. Thirteen years old and riding an outlaw – naturally I wanted only that. I wanted to indulge shamelessly my vanity, to drink the daring and success of my exploit in full-strength draughts, but Isabel, like a conscientious teacher at a fair, dragging you off to see instructive things, insisted on the landscape.

Look, she said firmly, while it's here before you, so that to the last detail it will remain clear. For you, too, some day there may be stalls and halters, and it will be a good memory.

But only for a moment or two, and then we were off again. She went even faster going home. She disdained and rebelled against her stall, but the way she whipped the wind around my ears you would have thought she had suddenly conceived a great affection for it. It was a strong wind, fiercely cold. There was a sharp sting in my ears a minute, then a sudden warmth and ease. I knew they were frozen, but there wasn't time to worry. I worked my collar up, crouched low again. Her mane blew back and lashed my face. Before the steady blast of wind my forehead felt as if the bone were wearing thin. But I didn't mind. I was riding her and holding on. I felt fearless, proud, mature. All the shame and misgivings of the past were over. I was now both her master and my own.

And then she was fifteen or twenty feet away, demurely watching me, and I was picking myself up and spitting snow.

She had done it with the utmost skill, right head first into a snowdrift, where I wouldn't hurt myself, less than a quarter of a mile from home.

And not even to toss her head and gallop off so that Millie would think she had done it in a fit of fright or meanness. Just to stand there, a picture of puzzled innocence, blandly transferring all the blame on me. What was wrong? Just when we were getting on so splendidly – why on earth had I deserted her?

For in her own way, despite her record, Isabel was something of a moralist. She took a firm stand against pride that wasn't justified. She considered my use of the word "master" insufferably presumptuous. Being able to ride an outlaw was not the same thing at all as being accorded the privilege of riding one, and for the good of my soul, it was high time I appreciated the distinction.

She stood still, sniffing in my direction, until I had almost reached her, then gave a disdainful snort and trotted pertly home. At the stable door she was waiting for me. I approached limping – not because I was hurt, but because with Millie standing back a little distance, goggle-eyed, I felt it looked better, made my tumble less an occasion for laughter – and as if believing me Isabel thrust her nose out, all condolence, and felt me tenderly where I was pretending it was sore. From the bottom of her heart she hoped I wouldn't be so unfortunate another time. So far as she was concerned, however, she could make no promises. There had been one fall, she explained to Millie, and there might easily be another. The future was entirely up to me. She couldn't be responsible for my horsemanship.

"Your ears are frozen," Millie changed the subject. "And your mother knows everything – she's going to let your father handle you."

I looked at her accusingly, but in a smug, self-righteous tone she explained, "She called you twice, and then came out to see why you didn't answer. Just in time to see it happen. I'll rub your ears with snow if you like before we go in for tea."

It was a good tea, but I didn't eat much. My ears were not only swelling badly and turning purple; they were also

starting to drip. My mother pinned a wash cloth to each shoulder, then sprinkled on talcum powder. She said nothing, but was ominously white-lipped and calm – saving herself up, I didn't doubt, until we were alone. I was in misery to escape upstairs to a mirror, but she insisted, probably as a kind of punishment, that I stay and finish my tea. Millie, I noticed, didn't eat much either, and kept her eyes turned fastidiously away.

When finally Mrs Dickson and Millie were gone – and as an additional humiliation, I wasn't allowed out to bring round their horse – my mother replaced the wash cloths with towels. Still silent, still white-lipped, and since there was no need, now that we were alone, for her to keep on saving herself up, it struck me that perhaps the condition of my ears was really serious.

"They're smarting bad – and throbbing," I said hopefully. "It must have been colder that I thought."

"It must have been," she agreed. "Go up to your room now out of my way till suppertime. I'd better talk to your father before he sees you anyway."

I knew then that she was as afraid of what was in store for me as I was. Her expression remained stern, but there was a softness in her voice, a note of anxiety. It was a good

139

sign, but it was also a bad one. It meant that she expected my father's anger to be explosive and extreme.

Upstairs, swollen and tender as they were, I gave my ears a brisk rubbing. They were already dripping and unsightly. A little worse, a darker, a more alarming purple, and they might get me out of a hiding.

While waiting I also rehearsed a number of entrances, a number of defences, but at the last minute abandoned all of them. The heat in my ears as I went downstairs was spreading like a prairie fire, and when I entered the kitchen there was such a blaze of it across my eyes that I could make out my father only as a vague, menacing form. A desperate resolve seized me; should he so much as threaten the razor strap I would ride away on Isabel and be lost to them forever.

But instead of pouncing he looked me over critically a minute, then hitched in his chair to the table and began buttering a piece of bread. "Some bronco buster," he said at last, in a weary, disillusioned voice. "All you need now is a ten-gallon."

"I didn't have the saddle – and she stopped short and shied." My voice climbed defensively. In dramatization of the suddenness of the stop I drove a clenched fist into an open palm. "I had been sticking on all right though – four miles or more."

"Anyway," he said resignedly, "you've got yourself a pretty pair of ears."

I raised a quick, self-conscious hand to touch them, and my mother assured me, "They're still there all right – don't worry. They made a hit with Millie too, judging by the look on her face. I think she'll be seeing them tonight in her sleep."

"But the mare," my father interrupted in a man-to-man tone of voice, abruptly cold-shouldering my mother, "how did you find her? Mean as she's supposed to be?"

"Not mean at all. Even when I was getting on – she stood and let me."

"Next time, just the same, you'd better play safe and use a snaffle. I'll hunt one up for you. It won't hurt her so long as she behaves."

"The next time!" my mother cried. "Talking about the next time when you ought to be taking down his breeches. She's no fit horse for a boy. If nobody'll buy her you ought to give her away, before she breaks somebody else's neck."

She went on a long time like that, but I didn't pay much attention. Pride – that was what it amounted to – pride even greater than mine had been before I landed in the snowdrift. It sent me soaring a minute, took my breath away, but it also brought a little shiver of embarrassment and shame. How long, then, had I kept them waiting? How many times in the last few months had they looked at me and despaired?

"One thing," my mother declared with finality, "you're not riding her to school. The things I'd be thinking and seeing all day – I just couldn't stand it."

"You hear," my father agreed. "I'll not have you carrying on with a lot of young fools crazy as yourself – being a good fellow, like as not, and letting them all ride her."

I was about to protest – as if any of them dared or could ride Isabel – but instead, remembering in time, went on docilely with my supper. Outwardly impassive, I was sky-high within. Just as Isabel herself had always said, what a sensation to ride foaming up to school at a breakneck, hair-raising gallop. In the past I had indulged the protest sparingly. Indeed, with so many threats and warnings in my ears, it had never been a prospect at all, but only a fantasy, something to be thought about wishfully, like blacking both Johnny Olsen's eyes at once, or having five dollars to spend. Now, though, everything was going to be different. Now, in their peculiar parental idiom, they had just given their permission, and Isabel and the future were all mine. Isabel and Millie Dickson. In accompaniment to a fervent resolve to be worthy of them both, my ears throbbed happily.

PHANTOM HORSE
COMES HOME

CHRISTINE PULLEIN-THOMPSON

*Phantom has been running wild in the Blue Ridge Mountains of
Virginia; Jean finds him dying and leads him home. Phantom
recovers and is tamed. But when Jean takes him to his first show he
refuses to enter the ring and bolts. It is then that a bet for five
hundred dollars is made between Jean and Mr Miller that Phantom
will never enter a ring. In this excerpt, Jean, her brother Angus and
their parents are back in England, and Mr Miller and his family
have come to stay.*

T HE WEATHER WAS FINE when I climbed out of bed at
five o'clock, stopping to pray for one brief moment
that Phantom would enter the ring and not let me
down. Outside the sun was rising above the trees. Phantom
was lying down, looking like a prince, with Mermaid
watching over him.

He let me put on a headcollar before he stood up and
shook himself. Cocks were crowing everywhere and there
was a continuous chorus of birdsong from the trees. The
grass was still wet and my jeans were soaked up to the
knee by the time I had reached the stable. Outside the road
was empty. The whole countryside at this moment seemed
to belong to me and the birds and, of course, Phantom.

At seven o'clock I was eating breakfast in the kitchen.

Phantom was plaited by this time. When I was struggling into my jodhpur boots Angus appeared from the summer-house looking sleepy in his pyjamas with a cobweb in his hair.

"Do you want any help? Have you got everything? Don't let us down." he said.

"I'll try. I'll do my best," I answered grimly.

Riding along the road towards the riding school I felt panic coming back. I must think of something else, of school, of Mermaid in foal; but I couldn't. I could only imagine Mr Miller waiting for his money. The post van was coming down the road now and I could see cows being turned into a meadow after milking. Phantom was carrying himself marvellously. I felt as though we were trotting on air.

The trailer was waiting in the yard, its ramp down, when I reached the riding school. Miss Mackintosh appeared in breeches and boots, white shirt, tie and hairnet. "It's going to be a glorious day," she said. "I'll load mine first."

She led out a big chestnut with two white socks behind. I wondered how she mounted so big a horse, as she led him towards the trailer. Three minutes later I was leading Phantom up the ramp, talking to him, saying, "This is our great day. You must behave."

Miss Mackintosh put the ramp up. "So far, so good," she said. "I'll just get my hat and coat and then we're off."

"Mum and Dad are bringing oats and grooming things," I said, putting my saddle and bridle in Miss Mackintosh's Land-Rover.

I sat in the front. The journey took an hour or more and was uneventful, except that I had a pain now in my right side and my legs had started to feel like jelly.

The show was in a stadium; there were no green trees, no open space. Only the trains tearing along a track fifty yards away, and tarmac, and dusty earth and cars. "No one told me it was here," I cried. "Phantom will never go in. He will think it's a trap. Why didn't someone tell me it was in a stadium?"

"It was on the schedule," replied Miss Mackintosh.

"It must have been in jolly small letters then," I said.

"Keep calm and he'll keep calm," suggested Miss Mackintosh. She was riding her chestnut in the Novice Jumping for Grade C Horses. I left Phantom in the trailer and watched the hacks being judged. The sun was shining and there were only a few people in the tiers of seats round the stadium. After a time I unboxed Phantom and tied him to the outside of the trailer and polished him with the stable rubber. I was feeling sick now. I simply couldn't imagine Phantom going into the stadium. I tacked up and walked him up and down, letting him look at everything. My class was at ten-thirty and the fourteen and under jumping was in progress. Phantom was too big for it.

I had never ridden in so large a show before. I cursed myself for entering without reading the front of the schedule and found myself longing for the small, cosy gymkhanas at which I had competed so often on Moonlight; where the first prize was three pounds and everyone knew everyone else.

But now my parents and Angus and the Millers had arrived. "Some show," shouted Wendy.

"Phantom looks great, and so do you," called Pete, no doubt trying to make up for the unpleasantness of the evening before. They looked very American, and I think quite a few people immediately decided I was American too.

"If you think Phantom's going in that stadium you're even nuttier than I ever imagined," Mr Miller told me.

I shrugged my shoulders. Secretly I agreed with him – it seemed impossible that Phantom would ever canter round the green turf with the people watching on all sides – but I wasn't going to let Mr Miller know. I was determined to keep the pretence up till the last minute of defeat.

Dad was wearing cotton trousers and a checked shirt. He patted Phantom and said quietly, "Don't let us down, Jean. Ride as though our lives depended on it."

The pain seemed to be growing in my side now and the winner of the fourteen and under jumping was coming out of the ring with a cup in her hand. If only it was over, I thought, if only I could go home and bury my head in some sand and never see the Millers again.

Now men were putting up the jumps. There were eleven of them and they were going up to three foot six at least.

"You look a bit green," said Angus glancing at me with a nervous smile lurking behind his eyes. "Shall I lead him up to the entrance when the moment comes?"

"If you like." I was feeling indifferent, somehow removed from it all now. I think that I simply couldn't face the suspense any more and had temporarily switched some part of myself off.

"They are calling you into the collecting ring," Mum told me. "All the luck in the world, darling."

She was wearing a suit and sling-back shoes.

"The same from here," cried Mrs Miller. "And don't you go worrying about Charlie's bet. Heavenly day, we don't expect you to pay five hundred dollars."

"I won't pay because I'm going in But anyway I always pay my debts."

Brave words! They seemed to come from a long way off. It wasn't really me speaking, but someone else, some ancestor braver than myself speaking for me.

I told the collecting-ring steward my number. It was thirteen.

"Thirteen!" shouted Wendy. "Gee whizz!"

Angus held Phantom while I walked the course. Surveying the jumps I felt sicker every second. There was a terrible combination of three, an enormous wall, a spread of parallel bars which seemed wider than any jump I had ever imagined and finally, a water jump. If it wasn't for the five hundred dollars I would be happy to remain outside, I thought, mounting again.

"Some jumps," Wendy said. "They sure look big – like Madison Square Garden."

I started to talk to Phantom. "We are going in there," I said. "It isn't a corral, there's nothing to worry about. Look, ponies are going in and coming out without any trouble; there's nothing to it." People were looking at me now but I ignored them. Phantom cocked an ear back and listened. I can't remember all I said, I just continued in the same voice, talking and stroking his neck.

Angus pulled off his tail bandage. "You're next," he said. "Good luck."

The collecting steward said, "Ready? All right, go in, but wait for the bell."

I could see the crowd in tiers of seats round the ring. Mr Miller was out there somewhere watching, so were Mum and Dad. Phantom was walking forward now, calmly, his neck arched. He played with his bit and dropped his nose and suddenly we were in the ring, trotting round waiting for the bell, and all my fear had gone, to be replaced by a feeling of immense confidence.

I prayed for the bell to ring soon and it did. I closed my legs against Phantom's sides and we were cantering towards the first jump. Phantom slowed down and for one terrible moment I thought, he's going to refuse, and it was something he had never done before. Then it was behind us and we were cantering towards the next fence, a road-closed sign, and now he was taking over. He didn't hesitate. In mid-air he seemed to kick his hind legs even higher and then we were racing on towards the parallel bars. After that came the wall, the gate, the fearsome combination where he took off too early for the last fence and scraped the top and there was an "Oh" from the crowd, but it didn't fall. There were crossbars and a stile and another jump I hardly noticed, then there was only one more jump now before the water. I slowed him down a little and then we were over that too, racing towards the water and I thought, don't let go yet, Jean, you're nearly clear, steady, steady, and then we were over and from the stands came a tremendous burst of clapping and I fell forward on Phantom's neck, patting him and saying over and over again, "We've done it."

"You're the only clear round so far," cried Angus, rushing to meet me.

"It was great," cried Pete. "You've won the bet."

"Doggone it, as if she doesn't know," cried Wendy.

A voice quite near said, "They're Americans. They must have come over especially. I bet she ends up jumping for the United States."

"Actually I'm English," I said turning round. "These are my friends from America. If I jump for any country it will be England."

They looked embarrassed.

"There's a jump-off," Dad said. "Well done, Jean."

Mr Miller held out an envelope. "It's yours, Jean," he told me. "You've sure earned it."

I didn't know what to say. At last I managed, "It's too much. You've done so much for us already."

"Exactly," agreed Dad trying to push away his hand.

"I pay my debts," replied Mr Miller. "This girl was prepared to sell the family silver and her jewellery for hers. I sure don't have to."

"Please don't, Charlie," pleaded Mum.

"Take it, Jean," shouted Mr Miller, pushing it into my hand. "And don't ever let it be said that Virginians don't pay their gambling losses."

"They are putting up the jumps," Angus said. "You'll be going first in the jump-off."

I rode in with the five hundred dollars in my pocket. Phantom danced a little and looked at the crowds, as though this time he knew they were there watching him. Then the bell sounded and we were cantering towards the first fence and as he jumped I suddenly knew what I would spend the dollars on – a horse for Angus who was standing now in the wings watching, a stable rubber in his hand. Phantom knocked the next fence, probably because my mind wasn't with him, for at that moment I was seeing a new horse coming to live at Sparrow Cottage.

The course was six inches higher except for the water-jump which remained the same, but I didn't notice it. We went faster this time and Phantom raced over the combination with a tremendous flourish as if to make up for rapping a fence last time. And now again we were racing for the water, and I sensed the tenseness of the crowd, the sudden hushed silence, which was quiet enough to let me hear the drone of an aeroplane overhead. Phantom took off too early, but it didn't matter for he had no intention of getting his hoofs wet. There was a burst of applause and I knew we were clear. I put my reins in one hand and cantering out, I could hear a train and Angus yelling, "Well done."

This time Miss Mackintosh was there to greet me too.

"What an achievement" she cried. "Well done, Jean."

I leapt off to find oats in my pockets for Phantom. The other clear round was going in now – a boy on a chestnut as lean as himself.

"Don't hurry him, let him look," said his mother, small and plump in dark glasses.

"It was a pity you hit the second fence," said Miss Mackintosh. "What happened?"

I remembered that she had always been keen on post-mortems. "I was thinking of something else," I said.

She made a tut-tutting noise.

The sun was shining on us all now and I longed to take off my coat. We could not see the whole ring, but someone said, "He's over the first three clear."

Angus started twisting the stable rubber into knots and biting his nails. A voice said, "Is your horse for sale? Because if he is, I would like to make an offer."

I shook my head and turned to see a military-looking man running his sharp eyes over Phantom. "I'll give you four thousand."

"He's not for sale. I'm keeping him forever," I said.

"He's hit the combination, he's stopped, the boy's falling off," shouted Angus. "You've won."

The Millers were running down the steps from the

stands. The boy was coming out leading his chestnut. Angus was jumping up and down. "Number Twenty-five has been eliminated," announced the loudspeaker.

Angus pulled up my girths. Dad started stroking Phantom's neck. Mum said, "You've won."

Pete said, "Holy smoke! I never knew he could jump like that. You wait till I tell them back home."

"They won't believe you," I replied, suddenly seeing the valley again in my imagination – the parched earth, the mountains in the distance, the Millers' house, the people saying, "Sure, but we don't believe you. That little horse will never make good, no siree."

"Oh yes they will," answered Pete. "I've got it all here real good. I brought a roll of film. I'll be sending it to the newspapers. I'll let the whole of Virginia know."

I wanted to say, "You're fantastic," but at that moment the loudspeaker announced, "Will the following numbers come into the ring: Number Thirteen. Miss Jean Simpson on Phantom . . ." I was riding in now and somewhere a band was playing. Phantom danced and tossed his head and I kept remembering the first time I had seen him galloping wild and alone across the moonlit valley. It all seemed to have happened years ago. I halted in the centre of the ring and the boy on the chestnut stopped beside me, and the band was still playing and the sun still shining and it was one of those golden moments which you never forget.

Everything seemed possible now, jumping for England, riding at Madison Square Garden in New York, doing the American circuit, all the big shows in the United States, and Canada – Toronto, Montreal. And now we were cantering round and I could see the Millers and Mum and Dad and Angus waiting outside, and nothing mattered now but the feel of the turf beneath us and Phantom's effortless canter which felt as though it could last for ever, through countless rings, round Badminton, through days and days of hunting, for half my life at least.

ANIMAL FARM

GEORGE ORWELL

When the animals rebel and take over Manor Farm, they hope for a better life. They decide that all animals will be equal. But soon the pigs become the new masters. Napoleon, the cleverest, is proclaimed President. Boxer, a kindly horse of almost eighteen hands, works harder than any of the other animals. Clover, a mare, and Benjamin, a wise old donkey, are his friends. Muriel is a white goat and Squealer is a treacherous pig.

AFTER HIS HOOF HAD healed up, Boxer worked harder than ever. Indeed, all the animals worked like slaves that year. Apart from the regular work of the farm, and the rebuilding of the windmill, there was the schoolhouse for the young pigs, which was started in March. Sometimes the long hours on insufficient food were hard to bear, but Boxer never faltered. In nothing that he said or did was there any sign that his strength was not what it had been. It was only his appearance that was a little altered; his hide was less shiny than it had used to be, and his great haunches seemed to have shrunken. The others said, "Boxer will pick up when the spring grass comes on", but the spring came and Boxer grew no fatter. Sometimes on the slope leading to the top of the quarry, when he braced his muscles against the weight of some vast boulder, it seemed that nothing kept him on his feet except the will to continue. At such times his lips were seen to form the words, "I will work harder"; he had no voice left. Once again Clover and Benjamin wanted him to take care of his health, but Boxer paid no attention. His twelfth birthday was approaching. He did not care what happened so long as a good store of stone was accumulated before he went on pension.

Late one evening in the summer, a sudden rumour ran round the farm that something had happened to Boxer. He had gone out alone to drag a load of stone down to the windmill. And sure enough, the rumour was true. A few minutes later two pigeons came racing in with the news: "Boxer has fallen! He is lying on his side and can't get up!"

About half the animals on the farm rushed out to the knoll where the windmill stood. There lay Boxer, between the shafts of the cart, his neck stretched out, unable even to raise his head. His eyes were glazed, his sides matted with sweat. A thin stream of blood had trickled out of his mouth. Clover dropped to her knees at his side.

"Boxer!" she cried. "How are you?"

"It is my lung," said Boxer in a weak voice. "It does not matter. I think you will be able to finish the windmill without me. There is a pretty good store of stone accumulated. I had only another month to go in any case. To tell you the truth, I had been looking forward to my retirement. And perhaps, as Benjamin is growing old too, they will let him retire at the same time and be a companion to me."

"We must get help at once," said Clover. "Run, somebody, and tell Squealer what has happened."

All the other animals immediately raced back to the farmhouse to give Squealer the news. Only Clover remained, and Benjamin, who lay down at Boxer's side, and, without speaking, kept the flies off him with his long tail. After about a quarter of an hour Squealer appeared, full of sympathy and concern. He said that Comrade

Napoleon had learned with the very deepest distress of this misfortune to one of the most loyal workers on the farm, and was already making arrangements to send Boxer to be treated in the hospital at Willingdon. The animals felt a little uneasy at this. Except for Mollie and Snowball, no other animal had ever left the farm, and they did not like to think of their sick comrade in the hands of human beings. However, Squealer easily convinced them that the veterinary surgeon in Willingdon could treat Boxer's case more satisfactorily than could be done on the farm. And about half an hour later, when Boxer had somewhat recovered, he was with difficulty got on to his feet, and managed to limp back to his stall, where Clover and Benjamin had prepared a good bed of straw for him.

For the next two days Boxer remained in his stall. The pigs had sent out a large bottle of pink medicine which they had found in the medicine chest in the bathroom, and Clover administered it to Boxer twice a day after meals. In the evening she lay in his stall and talked to him, while Benjamin kept the flies off him. Boxer professed not to be sorry for what had happened. If he made a good recovery, he might expect to live another three years, and he looked forward to the peaceful days that he would spend in the corner of the big pasture. It would be the first time that he had had leisure to study and improve his mind. He intended, he said, to devote the rest of his life to learning the remaining twenty-two letters of the alphabet.

However, Benjamin and Clover could only be with Boxer after working hours, and it was in the middle of the day when the van came to take him away. The animals were all at work weeding turnips under the supervision of a pig, when they were astonished to see Benjamin come galloping from the direction of the farm buildings, braying at the top of his voice. It was the first time that they had ever seen Benjamin excited – indeed, it was the first time that anyone had ever seen him gallop. "Quick, quick!" he shouted. "Come at once! They're taking Boxer away!" Without waiting for orders from the pig, the animals broke off work and raced back to the farm buildings. Sure enough, there in the yard was a large closed van, drawn by two horses, with lettering on its side and a sly-looking man in a low-crowned bowler hat sitting on the driver's seat. And Boxer's stall was empty.

The animals crowded round the van. "Good-bye, Boxer!" they chorused, "good-bye!"

"Fools! Fools!" shouted Benjamin, prancing round them and stamping the earth with his small hoofs. "Fools! Do you not see what is written on the side of that van?"

That gave the animals pause, and there was a hush. Muriel began to spell out the words. But Benjamin pushed her aside and in the midst of a deadly silence he read:

"'Alfred Simmonds, Horse Slaughterer and Glue Boiler, Willingdon. Dealer in Hides and Bone-Meal. Kennels Supplied.' Do you not understand what that means? They are taking Boxer to the Knacker's!"

A cry of horror burst from all the animals. At this moment the man on the box whipped up his horses and the van moved out of the yard at a smart trot. All the animals followed, crying out at the tops of their voices. Clover forced her way to the front. The van began to gather speed. Clover tried to stir her stout limbs to a gallop, and achieved a canter. "Boxer!" she cried. "Boxer! Boxer! Boxer!" And just at this moment, as though he had heard the uproar outside, Boxer's face, with the white stripe down his nose, appeared at the small window at the back of the van.

"Boxer!" cried Clover in a terrible voice. "Boxer! Get out! Get out quickly! They are taking you to your death!"

All the animals took up the cry of "Get out, Boxer, get out!" But the van was already gathering speed and drawing away from them. It was uncertain whether Boxer had understood what Clover had said. But a moment later his face disappeared from the window and there was the sound of a tremendous drumming of hoofs inside the van.

He was trying to kick his way out. The time had been when a few kicks from Boxer's hoofs would have smashed the van to matchwood. But alas! his strength had left him; and in a few moments the sound of drumming hoofs grew fainter and died away. In desperation the animals began appealing to the two horses which drew the van to stop. "Comrades, comrades!" they shouted. "Don't take your own brother to his death!" But the stupid brutes, too ignorant to realize what was happening, merely set back their ears and quickened their pace. Boxer's face did not reappear at the window. Too late, someone thought of racing ahead and shutting the five-barred gate; but in another moment the van was through it and rapidly disappearing down the road. Boxer was never seen again.

Three days later it was announced that he had died in the hospital at Willingdon, in spite of receiving every attention a horse could have. Squealer came to announce the news to the others. He had, he said, been present during Boxer's last hours.

"It was the most affecting sight I have ever seen!" said Squealer, lifting his trotter and wiping away a tear. "I was

at his bedside at the very last. And at the end, almost too weak to speak, he whispered in my ear that his sole sorrow was to have passed on before the windmill was finished. `Forward, comrades!' he whispered. `Forward in the name of the Rebellion. Long live Animal Farm! Long live Comrade Napoleon! Napoleon is always right.' Those were his very last words, comrades."

Here Squealer's demeanour suddenly changed. He fell silent for a moment, and his little eyed darted suspicious glances from side to side before he proceeded.

It had come to his knowledge, he said, that a foolish and wicked rumour had been circulated at the time of Boxer's removal. Some of the animals had noticed that the van which took Boxer away was marked "Horse Slaughter", and had actually jumped to the conclusion that Boxer was being sent to the knacker's. It was almost unbelievable, said Squealer, that any animal could be so stupid. Surely, he cried indignantly, whisking his tail and skipping from side to side, surely they knew their beloved Leader, Comrade Napoleon, better than that? But the explanation was really very simple. The van had previously been the property of the knacker, and had been bought by the veterinary surgeon, who had not yet painted the old name out. That was how the mistake had arisen.

The animals were enormously relieved to hear this. And when Squealer went on to give further graphic details of Boxer's death-bed, the admirable care he had received, and the expensive medicines for which Napoleon had paid without a thought as to the cost, their last doubts disappeared and the sorrow that they felt for their comrade's death was tempered by the thought that at least he had died happy.

Napoleon himself appeared at the meeting on the following Sunday morning and pronounced a short oration in Boxer's honour. It had not been possible, he said, to bring back their lamented comrade's remains for internment on the farm, but he had ordered a large wreath to be made from the laurels in the farmhouse garden and sent down to be placed on Boxer's grave. And in a few days' time the pigs intended to hold a memorial banquet in Boxer's honour. Napoleon ended his speech with a reminder of Boxer's two favourite maxims, "I will work harder" and "Comrade Napoleon is always right" – maxims, he said, which every animal would do well to adopt as his own.

On the day appointed for the banquet, a grocer's van drove up from Willingdon and delivered a large wooden crate at the farmhouse. That night there was the sound of uproarious singing, which was followed by what sounded like a violent quarrel and ended at eleven o'clock with a tremendous crash of glass. No one stirred in the farmhouse before noon on the following day, and the word went round that from somewhere or other the pigs had acquired the money to buy themselves another case of whisky.

MIDNIGHT STALLION

PATRICIA LEITCH

I USED TO CUT OUT photographs of Thoroughbred horses, pin them up on my bedroom walls and dream that they were mine; that they grazed in my paddocks and stood in my stables waiting to be saddled, bridled and ridden out over the stretches of sand that lay below our farm.

Sand that reached as far as the eye could see. Sand that was almost white, glistening with a pearl sheen under the moon as the tide drew back – a dancing floor for the white mares of Poseidon.

The mares with manes of foam, who came thundering in night after night as I lay curled in my bed listening to them; white sea-green mares who left no footprints behind them.

I used to search for their hoofprints. Finding them would have been the magical sign I was always seeking. A sign to tell me that I, Kate Flann, was different; that I would not grow up to become a shop assistant or a typist or, worse of all, be trapped in the drudgery of the farm like my mother. Our farm, with its wind-flattened crops, scrawny cattle, decaying walls and leaking roof, was a prison.

159

I searched for a sign that somehow I would find my way into the world of horses. I would work in racing stables with those high, proud horses.

The speed of them, the blaze of them would be mine. But in our harsh, dead farm I only knew their paper ghosts and no matter how hard I searched I found no magic hoofprints.

The only hoofprints on the sands were those of Peggotty, the farm pony. She was as sour and crabby as the mist that rolled in from the sea, filling our lives with its damp breath.

During the winter my father sat by the kitchen fire, in the summer by the farm door, his bony, lantern-jawed face empty, his flat blue eyes staring inward. Bird-boned as myself, he stretched out his sparrow legs, pulled his cap down over his eyes with delicate, conscious hands and ignored my mother's nagging.

I hardly knew my silent father. He sat drinking black tea, smoking his pipe, crouched over some unspeakable secret from his past, while my mother cleaned and washed, fed beasts and hens and, almost as soon as I had pinned them up, pulled down my paper horses and burnt them.

She would have no such nonsense in her house. Gambling and racing were the devil's playthings. But my favourite horses were hidden from her passionate destruction, only the sea mists knew their rafter security.

Before Tim, my elder brother, abandoned us forever he came into the stable where I was brushing caked mud off Peggotty and told me he was going to sea. I wasn't to tell our parents until he'd gone. He was broad-shouldered and tall like my mother, not a flicker of anything like my father and myself.

A mote-dense beam of sunlight streamed through the broken stable window blotting him out. My eyes were filled with tears at the cruelty of his courage in leaving the farm; his unlikely kindness in telling me he was going. I

could hardly see him. I asked my question into a dazzle of light that divided us.

"What did he do?" I asked, feeling the ground tremble, the stable walls collapse about me for I had put into words the question that could not be asked; that must never be mentioned between any of us.

"The old man?" Tim said, as if I could possibly have meant anyone else. His voice was suddenly polite, false, and I was terrified that he wasn't going to tell me.

"What did he do?" I demanded. "Before he came to the farm and married Mam?" The farm had belonged to my mother. Its barren acres, perched on the edge of nowhere, only to be reached by miles of rutted track, had been handed down through four generations of her family.

"It was the horses," said my brother.

"Horses? What was he doing with horses?" I asked, not lifting my eyes.

"Did you not know?" he said knowing that I didn't. "It's the jockey he was before the trouble."

I had not known, Had not known that my father had ridden the bright, blood horses of my dreams.

"Trouble?"

"He was done for doping them. Him and the trainer."

"Prison?"

"He got off. But it finished him. He didn't ride again."

"Was he telling you himself?"

"He was not. It was a bit in an old paper that told me. Guilty it said he was, had it not been for the grand friends that bought him out of it."

Tim had been away for almost a year, when I saw the horse box coming along the farm track. It was a spring evening with air so sweet that even Peggotty had the breath of it and was allowing herself to be cantered in circles jagged as a rocking horse, but without her usual bouts of bucking and swallow-swooping shies against her ribs.

In the distance of the hilly track the horse box rose and fell as it came towards the farm. It was a ramshackle thing with wooden sides held together by a cross hatching of planks. Peggotty flung up her head and sent her raucous mare's bray blurting up the cliffside.

From the box came an imperious, dominant answer; a sound I had never heard before.

I took Peggotty's bridle off and then crept slowly round the corner of the hay shed where I could watch the yard without being seen.

Two men were speaking to my father. One was short and stout with a whisky-bloomed face. The other was lean, ginger-sharp and although the clothes he wore were faded and folded about his long bones you could see at once there was quality in them.

"It would be for the one night only," said the little, beacon man. "We'll be back for him tomorrow and not a soul the wiser. And for yourself . . ."

From his pocket he brought out a thick wad of money.

"I will not," said my father. "With the entire police force of Ireland on your trail for all I know."

"Not a one has a breath of us. We have him clean away and not a soul to know that it was himself winning today and not the old crock they thought was running."

"I will not." said my father again and I thought he would turn and leave them.

"It's the short memory you have, Pat Flann," said the tall man.

My mother came to the farm door, stood with her arms folded over her coarse apron. She stood staring at the three men then, without a word, turned and went back inside, slamming the door shut behind herself. From inside the box came the trample of hooves, the high, nickering whinny and then a full-flung explosion of hind feet against the tawdry wood.

"But there's some have not forgotten the money they lost," said the tall, fox-featured man casually. "Some who would still be interested to know where they could find you. And some who could tell them."

They turned and walked away from me so that I couldn't hear what they were saying, but from their backs it looked to me as if the tiny figure of my father stood between two jailers, a prisoner in his own yard. I heard the short man laugh and although my father pushed the wad of notes away I knew from the way the tall man laid his hand on my father's shoulder that he had agreed to do what they wanted.

They backed the box into the dark cell that had once been the bull pen, so I could only hear their captive come crashing down the lowered ramp and the men's voices swearing.

When the men had driven away my father slid the bolt home, padlocked it securely and slipped the key into the breast pocket of his waistcoat.

I went to my room early that night leaving my father crouched over the fire, staring into the flames while my mother sat silently opposite.

I took down my box of paper horses from its rafter hiding place and sitting on my bed I turned over the photographs one by one. I drank them in, lost in their beauty while from the yard below there was the music of trampling hooves, the high, sweet calling. Calling me to come and ride.

It was the early morning before my father's snoring settled into a regular pattern and I knew it was as safe as it would ever be.

I lifted the latch on my bedroom door, and stood barefoot on the landing, my shoes in my hand. My silent feet tested each step of the stairs before I settled my feather weight into the wood.

I crossed the kitchen. Fear of waking my father tightened at my heart as my fingers felt into the egg cup that sat on the left hand corner of the dresser. The padlock key swam into my hand, twin to the one that my father had slipped into his pocket.

A full moon raced motionless through wind-blown clouds as I sat on the back doorstep tying on my shoes. I crossed the yard and took Peggotty's bridle from where I had left it and went slowly, slowly, on to the bull pen where I stood in front of the padlocked doors, the key in my hand.

It was not fear that held me back as I stood on the brink of my miracle. It was a kind of wonder. Not wonder at what was about to happen but wonder that I should ever have been so stupid as to think it might not happen.

I turned the key in the padlock, slid back the bolt and went in, the door closing behind me. The black stallion stood in the far corner, his body lost in darkness. His head, turned towards me, was caught in a net of moonlight that fell through the grill set high in the stone wall, revealing a white blaze, dark ears sharp above a wisped forelock, glistening, moon-mirroring eyes, nostrils trembling with challenge and fine, sensitive lips, As he moved towards me I held out my hand, hardly breathing.

He circled me, neck stretched, silken tail switching about his muscled quarters and over his steel-boned hocks. He

aimed one snaking, reaching kick then relaxed. I laid my hand on his neck and it was hard as living rock. I reached to his crested mane and stroked the bulging mass of his shoulder and the plateau of his back. All the time I was talking to him – whispering, words almost without meaning. Only the sound of my voice told him that he came from my dreams.

I took down the rope halter, hooked by the manger – Peggotty's bridle was a useless frivolity. He lowered his head and I slipped it over his ears, secured the rope round his muzzle and, holding him by its length, we went out into the yard and down the track to the beach.

He flaunted at my side, every step he took was tight sprung with energy. Yet he did not trot but kept to his spring-hooved, flirting walk. The track opened to the sea, to a line of breakers far out over moon-blanched sands. For a split second he stood poised, perfectly still, the sea wind bannering back mane and tail, sleeking the moon-shadowed contours of his face. In that second I sprang to his shoulder, and clutching mane and rope I was astride him when he launched into freedom.

He reared, landed, flung his hooves in crazed piaffes and cabrioles. He advanced to the sea mares, flirting in their wind-blown shadows, blowing into their arching manes. Then the flat, reaching sands took the wildness of his eyes. A limitless racecourse where he could race against only himself and the wind stallions.

I felt his whole being tighten as he drew back the bow of his speed. I knotted rope and silken strands of mane even tighter into my grip. He sprang forward, leaping over space as if the empty night air built barricades before him, then he stretched out, neck low, legs like pistons, his face drawn to the magnetic, invisible rim where sand and sky met.

He showed no sign that he was aware of me as I crouched over his withers like a ghost. It was all a daze of

glory, a bursting torrent of unleashed power. Silvered sea and sand skidded past my eyes. I rode free from the bonds of place or time, as I raced against the glimmering moon track that spread its glinting phosphorescent dance over the sea's surface.

A gull flew up out of the darkness and the horse swung round on his hocks and plunged back the way we had come. In that moment all Peggotty's sins were forgiven. It was only due to her twisted, unbroken resistance to all my attempts to school her that I was still astride the horse as he galloped back over his own moon-filled prints.

I was now aware of the world of my father's fury if he found out what I had done. If I had fallen and let the horse gallop loose, what would have happened then? I had to get him back to the farm before anyone found out.

I tried to sit up, to tug at the halter rope, to impose ludicrous control over his speed but he galloped on as if I had never moved. Would I race backwards and forwards over the same stretch of sand until my father discovered us? Again I yanked at the rope, pulling furiously with all my strength but the horse only shook his head, throwing me down onto his neck as he thundered on.

We had almost reached the track to the farm when

Peggotty's neighing bray shattered the night silence. The stallion stopped dead, chucking me to the ground. I ran at his side as he trotted up the track towards the sound.

In the yard he stopped and stared about him. His head held high, his white blaze like an uplifted lamp, he screamed into the night. Pathetically I tugged at the halted rope trying to turn him towards the bull pen but he paid as little attention to me as he had when I was on his back.

From the shadows of an outhouse a figure moved towards us. Without a word my father took the halter rope from me and in that instant the horse changed from the mythical, winged horse of my dream to an animal subject to man. He reared against my father's control and fought as he was led back to the prison of the bull pen; but he was an animal and went where he was taken.

My father worked about him, neat and sure in his movements – drying the sweated coat, cleaning legs and hooves, wiping the brilliant face. He spoke to the horse, not to me as I stood silently watching.

When the horse was groomed and pulling at hay he stood back, and I knew that in seconds the heavy doors of the bull pen would be closed and I would never see the horse again. In that moment my mind filled with madness. I would phone the police and tell them that I knew where the horse was; or I would hide in the horse box, go with the horse to make sure that no harm came to him.

The horse turned his head, looked full at me and in that moment I knew that there was nothing I could ever do for him. In his being he was not only free from his fate at the hands of the men who had brought him here; he was free also from my romantic obsession.

My father shut the doors, bolted and padlocked them. He walked behind me to the farm. At the farm door he paused.

"Be staying in your room," he said, "until the horse is away."

I nodded, opening the door, turning away from him so that he wouldn't see the tears trailing my cheeks.

I was at the foot of the stairs when I heard him catch his breath.

"When the time comes," he said, breaking the silence that had lain between us all my life, "if you still have the notion on you, I'll have a word with a trainer I know. He runs a good straight place and for old time's sake he'll take you on."

By the time I had taken in the meaning of his words, spun round to question him, he was into the kitchen brewing tea for himself, his back set against me.

At odd, sea-strolling moments I still look for the prints of the sea mares but they don't matter now. It didn't really matter when my mother sniffed out my cut-outs hidden in the rafters and threw them on the fire. For I, Kate Flann, have a father who will speak to a trainer for me.

My sign had been with me all the time.

SNOW TO THE RESCUE

GERALD RAFTERY

from Snow Cloud Stallion

Ken lives on a farm with his uncle and aunt in Vermont, USA. The unpredictable behaviour of his horse, Snow Cloud, is worrying Ken, but then the health of his aunt becomes a more serious concern.

WHEN THEY FINISHED the chores, Uncle Ira paused in the middle of the barnyard and pointed to the declining sun. "It's going to be a grey sunset. We're about due for a break in this hot spell."

After supper they sat on the porch for a while. The air was still and breathless; they could hear a dog barking a mile away at the Johnson place. Heat lightning played far off on the horizon, and the usual evening breeze did not spring up.

"When we get that storm, it's going to be a corker. It might even be tonight," said Uncle Ira.

Ken slept fitfully, his rest disturbed as much by the worry over Snow as by the heat. The hoped-for rain did not arrive, and in the morning it was still hot and sticky. As they went out to do the chores, the sunrise was red and angry. High threads of clouds were stretched across the sky.

171

"It's coming, all right," said Uncle Ira, shaking his head. "We won't get much work done today."

They got their own breakfast, and later Aunt Martha came down looking fresh and rested in spite of the heat.

"I guess Dr Smathers knew what was wrong," said Uncle Ira, smiling his satisfaction. "You do what he says and you'll be all right in a hurry."

"That was good medicine," said Aunt Martha. "I think I'll bake a batch of pies this morning."

"Now, you'll do nothing of the kind," began Uncle Ira, before he saw that she was laughing at him.

Ken felt a little more cheerful as they went out to work. Aunt Martha's improvement almost counter-balanced his worries about Snow. The day was still hot and sunny, but huge castle-like clouds were piling up on the horizon. There was not a breath of wind stirring the heavy air.

"We'll take the team down to that lower field and spread fertilizer," said Uncle Ira, casting a practised glance at the sky. "We might get a morning's work in before the storm."

He took turns with Ken, one driving while the other shovelled at the tail gate of the wagon. It was hot work and they looked longingly at the sky every few minutes. The clouds were moving in on the valley now. They could see the billowing peaks of the great piles as the tremendous air currents inside sent the tops boiling and reaching up towards the sun. Stopping to breathe the horses, they saw that the oncoming storm had topped the rim of the valley, half a dozen miles away. The summit of the mountain ridge vanished behind a veil of rain.

"There's going to be plenty of wind in that when it gets here," said Uncle Ira. "We'd better finish this up and get the team under cover."

They hurried down the length of the field, flinging shovels of fertilizer after them. The flying clouds had reached high enough to cover the sun, and the still air was cool and electric. Every time they looked up, the rushing veils of rain had slipped nearer down the sloping side of the valley. Lightning flickered through the black clouds above the rain.

The horses, sensing the coming storm, tossed their heads and stared around. Off in the distance could be heard the soft roar of the rain and the occasional rolling of thunder.

At last they turned towards the stable, the lightened wagon jouncing and jolting over the ground as Butch and Babe threw all their weight into the collars. A chilly gust of wind caught up with them and sent the horses' tails whipping against their flanks. A cold spatter of rain flickered across them.

Ken looked back. A flying scud of broken clouds was overhead, and the white curtain of the rain had reached the highway through the valley. He could see the tops of the trees lashing wildly in the wind and hear a steady roar from the storm. As he watched, a forked flash of lightning halted for an instant over a tree at the edge of the open meadow, and a splitting crash of thunder made him flinch. A huge leafy section toppled slowly out of the side of the tree and then hurtled to the ground, blocking the road that led down to the highway. Ken gripped Uncle Ira's shoulder and shouted to him.

The full force of the rain was upon them as they pounded into the barnyard. Ken leaped over the side of the wagon and ran to the horses' heads, holding them steady while Uncle Ira unhooked the traces. Together, with arms crooked over their faces, they led the horses through sheets of blinding rain to the stable door.

Inside, it seemed strangely quiet by comparison with the wild outdoors. There was a steady drumming of rain upon the roof, but the whistling of the wind seemed far away. Snow had come into the stable and he whinnied inquiringly as Butch and Babe tramped, dripping into the stalls.

Uncle Ira picked up a grain sack to hold over his head. "I'm going to run up to the house and help Martha close the windows. I'll be back in a minute and lend you a hand with the horses."

As he opened the door, the wind snatched it out of his hand and banged it against the wall of the stable. He ducked out into the slashing rain and slammed it behind him.

Ken began rubbing the horses dry with a piece of sacking. They had quieted down now that they were out of the rain and they seemed content to rest in the dimness of the stable. The rain drummed on the roof far overhead, and there was an occasional squealing of wind around the eaves.

Suddenly Ken stopped working. He listened hard. Was that a voice? Or was it the gurgling of the flooded rainspout? He walked out of the stall and stood listening at the closed door. Someone was calling him. He eased the door open against the wind and peered out. Uncle Ira stood on the porch, beckoning wildly. Ken ducked out and ran splashing through the puddles to the house.

Uncle Ira was white-faced and frightened. "Come on in!" he gasped. "Martha's had a heart attack."

Ken followed him into the house and closed the door to shut out the sound of wind and rain. "Did you call Dr Smathers?"

"I couldn't get an answer." He picked up the phone again and jiggled the hook, talking over his shoulder. "She was running around closing windows when she felt the pains. She got the medicine out, but her hands shook so she dropped the bottle. Right in the sink. It's smashed."

He broke off suddenly and spoke into the phone. "Dr Smathers - and hurry!" He said to Ken, "She's in bed now, but she looks awful peaked."

"Hello, Doc," he began, as the connection was made, and poured out his story.

Ken listened to him while the wind howled outside and rattled the windows of the darkened house. It was clear to him from one side of the conversation that the doctor could not come.

Uncle Ira protested for a moment, and then listened. "Yes, I did that, Doc!" He listened again. "Well, if we have to, I guess . . ."

A flash of lightning glared across the room and a sudden blast of thunder drowned out his words.

"Hello, hello! Doc!" Uncle Ira jiggled the hook again and then slowly replaced the receiver. "The line's dead; that last stroke must have brought a tree down on it."

They faced each other in silence for a moment across the quiet room.

"The doctor can't come!" Uncle Ira seemed suddenly very old and tired. "Trees are down across the road in the village and there's been a bad auto accident south of town. He was just starting out for that on foot. He says if we get in to his place his wife has the medicine there."

"We'd never get the car past that fallen tree on our road," said Ken.

Uncle Ira sat down and buried his face in his hands. The windows rattled as another blast of wind swept around the house like a hurricane. Torrents of rain slashed against the windows and drummed at the walls.

Ken paced the floor. The eight miles to town and back would take hours on foot in weather like this. Suddenly he reached a decision. He strode across the room and put a hand on his uncle's shoulder. "I'll saddle Snow and make a try for it. It's better than doing nothing."

Uncle Ira lifted a haggard face. "It's an awful chance. Snow'll run wild in a storm like this. You know how lightning scares a horse."

Ken was already in the kitchen, hauling a poncho out of the piled clothes rack. He pulled an oilskin cap down tight on his head.

His uncle followed him. "Watch out for falling branches. I remember how it was when the hurricane hit us up here in '44. Stick to the open fields where you can, no matter how heavy the rain is."

Ken nodded, and tightened his belt. With his hand on the knob of the door, he said, "I'll be back as quick as I can."

Outside, the wind came in gusts that took his breath away. He dashed for the stable through puddles that had swelled tremendously in the last few minutes. After he had closed the stable door, he paused for a moment to calm

himself and catch his breath. Snow would sense any nervousness or excitement; he would have to act as naturally as possible. He walked into the stall, forcing himself to move as slowly as he could. He patted the big stallion for a moment and then brought out the bridle from behind his back. Snow tossed his head happily and blew a soft snort of eagerness.

When Ken finally led the horse out of the stall, he paused for a moment before opening the door. He waited until Snow stirred restlessly and nickered before he swung the door wide into the storm. Then he stepped out quickly and slammed the door shut as soon as Snow sidestepped clear of it. He gave him no time to worry about the wind and rain. Putting his foot in the stirrup, he swung quickly up into the saddle.

Snow shied and jibbed a little at facing into the wind. He pranced nervously through the splashing puddles until they gained a little shelter from the bushes along the side of the yard. Ken waved an arm automatically to the empty windows as they passed the farmhouse and swung out into the road. Snow moved more surely now, and for a hundred yards or so he galloped easily and freely. Then the fallen tree loomed ahead, a huge leafy barrier. He flung up his head and slowed his pace, turning half away to look it over warily.

Ken leaned forward and talked to him, patting his neck and murmuring reassuringly. He let him slow down to a walk and approach the strange sight at his own speed. When he was reassured, Ken guided him off the road to circle the ruin of the shattered elm.

Out in the open field they felt the full force of the wind, and the driven rain pelted and stung like sand. Snow broke into a gallop and, with a clear open stretch before them, Ken let him have his head and run as he liked. Half a mile farther on they came to the belt of trees that bordered the little river into which Johnsons' brook flowed. The trees sheltered them from the wind for a minute, and Snow quieted down as they pounded across the wooden planks of the bridge.

Before them was the concrete highway. Ken turned left and kept Snow to the soft level footing on the shoulder of the road. There was no sign of traffic; the smooth surface was speckled with leaves and broken twigs. The horse had the wind at his side now and he went more willingly.

Ken relaxed for a moment and stared around. Suddenly, like the explosion of a giant flash bulb, came a dazzling flare of lightning and a simultaneous crash of thunder. Snow leaped forward in alarm. Ken was almost as frightened himself, and it was only the instinctive ducking forward of his head and the sudden tightening of his knees that kept him from losing his seat. Snow shot ahead like an arrow, running unrestrained in a mad panic for a hundred yards. Only the flood of rain, pouring down even more heavily than before, slowed him to a steadier pace.

A quarter of a mile farther on they encountered a new difficulty. Rounding a sharp curve on a sloping hillside, they came suddenly upon another fallen tree blocking the road. Beyond it, a truck had been halted. There was no room to pass, even for Snow.

Ken swung to the ground and passed the slippery reins forward over the horse's head. Snow shivered and stared about him with white-rimmed eyes, but he followed as Ken plunged downhill through dripping bushes below the upflung roots of the great tree. When they regained the road on the other side, Snow seemed a little less nervous. Ken stood in the rain for a moment to pat him before he swung into the saddle again.

As they passed the truck, he noticed that it was empty. Up on the hill-side he saw that the two men who had been riding in it had taken shelter in an open shed. They waved to him and he tossed up an arm in reply.

For a mile the road was open and empty and there was only the steady pelting of the rain to worry about. The wind was still fierce and strong, however, and ahead of them beyond the clear stretch there was a place where the road was lined on both sides with a heavy growth of trees. Ken slowed to a walk. He saw now how good Uncle Ira's advice had been. The treetops tossed and clashed in the wild gusts of wind, and the dark road under the trees was littered with leaves and twigs and whole branches.

Snow seemed to sense the danger. For the first time since they had started, he came to a full stop of his own accord. Ken stared around. There was no way to circle the wooded stretch. On one side the trees extended a quarter of a mile down to the river and on the other far up the mountainside. He patted Snow's neck and murmured an encouragement that he did not feel. They would have to go straight through the dim tree-shadowed stretch of road. The darkness of the storm made it seem even more murky and ominous.

Ken urged Snow forward under the trees. It was hard to resist the temptation to dash through it at full speed. He reined the horse firmly down to a steady trot and watched sharply for dangling limbs and falling branches overhead. Underneath the stormy canopy the rain and wind ceased to bother them, but there was a steady roaring through the storm-lashed treetops high above. Ken wiped the trickling rain from his face with a wet hand and stared at the leaky roof that stretched before him.

Once Snow shied and reared at a split branch hanging from a tree that shook and quivered alarmingly as the tree swayed in the wind. Ken soothed him with hand and voice and coaxed him past it.

The end of the grove was visible as a brightness on the road ahead when suddenly there was a fierce cracking and splintering sound almost directly above them. Ken did not pause to look. Almost by instinct he urged the stallion forward and slapped the reins loose on his neck. Snow quivered at the sound and sprang forward instantly in to a full gallop. Ken sensed rather than saw the huge bulk of a broken branch bearing down almost on his back. An instant later the crash of its fall sent Snow forward in uncontrolled flight.

The boy made no effort to restrain him, but leaned forward and murmured words of praise in a voice that he tried to keep calm. Running out his fright was the best thing for Snow under the circumstances. They flashed forward and in a few moments they were out in the storm again.

As they broke into the open, the rain and wind were upon them. The first gust caught Ken with his face raised to the sky; it tore the sou'wester cap from his head and sent it flying off into a field. He stared at it over his shoulder as it went spinning and rolling away before the wind. It would be more trouble than it was worth to go after it now.

In half a minute he missed it. There was rain in his eyes, and his soaked hair straggled down on his forehead. A steady trickle of water began running down the back of his neck. He lowered his head against the wind and peered ahead as Snow slowed to a trot. There was only a little more than a mile to go, and he might be able to cut that down a bit. The highway took a long sweeping curve into the village. He could leave it and cut across the open fields without too much trouble. He ran over the route in his mind. There were only two fences and both had gates, but there was a narrow little brook. It might be swollen by the rain, but it would hardly be too deep for Snow to wade.

There was an open barway ahead. Ken tapped Snow's neck with the near rein and guided him into it. He could have sworn that the big horse gave a sigh of relief as he felt the soft ground under his hoofs and saw the clear fields ahead of him. The wind was almost at their backs now, which gave them some relief from the stinging rain. Snow broke into a long easy canter without any signal from his rider.

Now that there was no immediate danger, Ken found his mind turning to the purpose of his hazardous journey. Aunt Martha's illness had been a nagging worry at the back

of his mind through the whole ride and, now that he faced
it, he felt a stirring of real fear. Automatically, he urged
Snow into a full gallop.

They topped a little hill and saw the brook in the fold of
the field before them. It had widened unbelievably, but it
was still shallow. Snow swept down the slope and splashed
through it with no distaste at all. He laboured up the
farther hill and swung without any guiding rein towards
the wide gate. He stood breathing hard while Ken climbed
stiffly to the ground and threw the gate open. After they
had walked through and Ken was in the saddle again,
having closed the gate behind him, Snow set off at a trot, as
though he realized the need to hurry. Down the swale of
the field they passed a herd of miserable cows, bunched up
for shelter behind a little shed and dark with rain.

At the top of the next rise they caught their first glimpse
of the village houses. Snow moved up into a canter at the
sight and did not slow his pace until he reached the last
fence before the outskirts of the little settlement. When that
was behind them, Ken felt that his journey was half

completed. He headed across the field and in a couple of minutes was out once more upon the highway. Before him lay the main street. It was a battered shambles. Two huge trees were down across the pavement.

One had been completely torn up, and a wall of tangled roots and muddy earth rose twenty feet in the air at the end of the fallen trunk. The other had been broken off by the force of the wind at a point where it separated into two branches, and each of the huge limbs had fallen in a different way. One had smashed the porch of a house and the other lay angled across the road. A car which had narrowly escaped being struck stood empty on the lawn where the driver had swerved it.

Snow was uneasy in these strange surroundings. Although there was no human being in sight along the rain-swept street, he sensed that this was a closed-in place. He was tired, but he managed to dance and fling his head nervously around as they moved into town between the two rows of houses. Realizing that he was afraid, Ken swung to the ground at once and took him by the bridle. He talked soothingly over his shoulder to the big stallion as he led him down the street to the doctor's house. Snow went more willingly when he could see his master walking calmly before him.

Ken was stiff and sore from the effort of controlling the horse and tense from the strain of worry. He was glad to use his legs for a change and get a little circulation in his cramped muscles. He realized, too, how wet he was when he could feel the water squishing in his sodden shoes.

He turned into the doctor's driveway and looked for a place where he could keep Snow out of the rain while he went in for the medicine. There was an open shed that had been used for carriages once. He led the horse in and looped reins loosely on a nail. With a pat on the neck and a word of praise, he turned and hurried towards the house.

A STAR FOR A LADY

DIANA PULLEIN-THOMPSON

"A GOOD 'OSS" WAS, to George Ledbetter, like a bag of gold. In the reign of Queen Victoria there was at least one horse dealer in every town – and George was the meanest of them all.

Bow-legged from hours of riding, wrinkled-faced, with sharp blue eyes, a blob of a nose and dark, dank hair, he was half-English, half-Irish. His father had been a butcher, and from the age of six George had been in and out of his father's stables, an undersized boy, quick, quiet and crafty. He spoke little, and he was poor at school work, but he kept his eyes open and his ears alert, watching the farrier at work and listening to horse-talk.

By the time George was twenty-five, it was said that he knew every trick of his trade.

If a horse was permanently lame on one foreleg, for example, he would prick the other, so that, being lame on both legs, the horse could not limp. To an inexpert eye, it would then seem sound.

He would file down the teeth of old animals, to make them appear younger, and drug lively or vicious horses

183

with hemp or opium so that they seemed docile when buyers came to see them.

George dealt in most kinds of horses: hunters, ladies' hacks, vanners, carriage horses, tram and bus horses, ponies for governess carts, ponies for children, polo ponies – even donkeys now and then. And if they were good-looking, well, all the better. "Folk will always pay a bit extra for something easy on the eye," he used to say.

But one hot day in June, George stood frowning in his well-swept yard, looking critically at a lightly-made Irish mare he had bought two months earlier at a London auction.

"Dammit," he said to himself. "If only she were prettier she would make a fine lady's 'oss, but, as it is, she's a Plain Jane if ever there was one. She'll end up in a cab or at a livery stable, and I won't have made a penny.' He sent a grain of grit spinning across the cobbled yard with the toe of one of his black boots, which were laced up to meet his gaiters.

Tied to a ring in the brick wall, the mare turned her head this way and that, her dark eyes catching the sunlight. Bright bay with black points, sharp little ears, a dainty muzzle and neat hoofs, she had a delicate look about her, which had so far prevented possible buyers coming near to paying the hundred and sixty guineas George was asking. All the ladies who visited his yard, always in the company of gentlemen, had gone for the greys or the prettily-marked animals, turning down the Irish mare as soon as she was brought out of her stall and they observed her plainness.

"What she needs," George decided suddenly, "is a star – a white star right in the middle of her forehead. Then the ladies would be falling over each other to buy her. I could call her Starlight, that would please 'em, put her price up a tenner and she'd sell like lightning."

Smiling a little at this flash of inspiration, he put his hairy hands in his pockets, jingled two half-sovereigns together and called in a voice growing hoarse with overuse:

" 'Ere, 'Arry. Come on, look sharp!"

A stable boy of around twelve came running across the yard from the forage room, where he had been furtively chewing a wedge of tobacco. "Yessir!" He stood, looking down at the cobbles, a red-cheeked, sandy-haired, lean boy, with watery blue eyes and, in spite of his servility, a knowing look on his meagre face. It was the expression of a boy who has lived with the low and cunning from an early age and seen their ways. He trusted no one.

"That mare needs a star to set her off."

"Yessir."

"So, I want you to look slippy – slippy, d'ye hear? – and run down to Smithy and fetch out Bob Barton, if he ain't too busy. Tell 'im I've got some business to talk with 'im. You understand?"

"Yes mister."

"Sir. Don't you mister me, young scoundrel, or I'll be telling your father of you."

"Yessir!"

"Go on, then, what are you waiting for, eh?"

The boy ran off.

George smiled. He felt lord of his yard, and any sense of power pleased him. He went up to the mare, ran his hands down her legs. "Clean as a whistle," he muttered. "Not a blemish anywhere. Maybe two hundred guineas would be nearer the mark . . ."

Within fifteen minutes the stable boy came back with a giant of a man, black-haired and bearded, with big, scarred hands and a forty-five-inch chest.

"Mornin', Bob. Terrible 'ot, isn't it. Must be something 'orrible in that smithy of yours."

" 'Tis and all,' agreed Bob Barton in his deep, growling voice.

After George had described the star he felt was needed to make the Irish mare more saleable, Bob went back to his forge to fetch the necessary equipment.

"Been a long time since anyone asked me to make a star," he said on his return. "But I used to be a great 'and at it five or six years ago. Farmer Griffin was mighty pleased with one I put on 'is five-year-old 'unter. Made all the difference, 'e said – sold the 'oss for two hundred guineas a year later."

As he talked, he worked. First of all the two men put a twitch on the mare's lip, so that she couldn't move without causing herself a strange, unforgettable pain. Then Bob cut four holes in her skin, so making the approximate shape of a star. Then he brought out an ivory skewer, which he used to work the skin within the area marked by the four holes, so that it was lifted away from the mare's forehead. Next, he produced two short lengths of wire and passed these diagonally across under the skin, so that there was a piece sticking out of each hole. These ends he made fast with packthread.

The mare was now in great pain; she trembled from head to foot, rolled her eyes and broke into a fearful sweat. But each time she moved or kicked, George tightened the twitch, so taking her attention away from the work of Bob's large but nimble hands. Round and round went the packthread, binding these half-inch ends of wire, until at last Bob was satisfied. Then he made a plaster of pitch – or tar, as we call it nowadays – and stuck it on the contraption of wire and thread, and motioned to George to release the twitch.

"That should make a pretty mare of 'er," he said, collecting together his tools and thread.

"Back in 'er stall, 'Arry," said George to the boy, who had been watching with that dreadful knowing look on his face.

"Let 'er 'ave just a little water, and then we'll give 'er a bran mash."

Bob, who was basically a kind man, ran his hand down the mare's neck.

"There, my little sweet'eart. All over now . . . all done. We've made a real beauty of you. Treat her kindly, like," he said, turning to Harry. "It'll ache a little bit for a day or two, and she may feel a bit poorly."

Having seen a soldier's legs amputated without an anaesthetic in the Crimean War, he considered the mare's sufferings to be slight and bearable.

In fact, she spent three days, head to a wall, with a ceaseless throbbing between her eyes, while the bay hair between the wires died for lack of blood and fell out.

Then Bob Barton returned, came to her stall, pulled off the plaster of pitch, loosened the cord and removed the wire. And the skin and nerves felt so dead that the mare hardly moved.

"Steady now, my little darling, this will make it feel better," he crooned in his deep voice, which had quietened many a youngster frightened by the acrid smell of the smoke from its own hoofs.

Gently he poured a mixture of honey of roses and tincture of benzoin into each hole, then rubbed the rest on the area which the pitch had held fast.

"Beautiful job," he said, standing back a little to admire his handiwork. "Bring 'er out, 'Arry, where the light's better. I reckon she's 'ad enough of this stall during the past three days." He turned to George. "Of course, there's some as use caustic, but that often turns the place bald. This be bald now, but the grey 'airs will soon be growing, stimulated by the mixture."

"Well, I pay on results," George declared firmly, a cunning expression flitting across his face. "The better the star, the better the pay."

"You always were an 'ard man," the farrier said. "Right then, I'll be back in ten days."

The mare stood outside with her head low, dazed and dejected.

"Give 'er a trot up and back. Get the blood running round 'er," ordered George. "I've never known Bob Barton fail yet."

And within ten days, sure enough, the white hairs were sprouting, and the shape of the star could be clearly seen.

But the mare, who had never glimpsed her face in a mirror, knew nothing of this. She only knew that the pain was over, that her forehead felt different and that she longed for a gallop again, the turf under her hoofs, the wind in her mane and the fresh, sweet smell of the country around her.

July came, and the season of riding hacks in the Park was past, for most of the rich left London in mid-summer for airier places. But one day the head groom of a nobleman's stable came on the lookout for a lightweight horse for his master's daughter. A pretty mare, he wanted, with a look of breeding about her. He had known George Ledbetter years ago, when they had both been young men struggling to make their way, and he knew that George would not even attempt to deceive him.

They clapped a saddle on the mare and put Harry on top, for the boy could ride most animals, astride or sidesaddle – or facing the tail, for that matter – being agile as a monkey.

He showed off the mare's paces and galloped her hard, so that the head groom could see her wind was all right.

"With a bit more schooling, I reckon she'll do," the groom said eventually. "You've not tampered with her, other than the star, 'ave you? Miss Alice fancies an 'oss with a star, if it can't be a dapple grey."

"I warrant 'er sound in wind, limb and eye, and there's five gold sovereigns for you, Jack, if you can get me a hundred and ninety guineas," replied George Ledbetter, smiling his secretive smile at the thought of the profit he was about to make.

The deal was completed within three weeks; the bay mare went to roomier, lighter quarters in the nobleman's spacious yard. Bob Barton demanded, and received, two sovereigns for his work, and George Ledbetter started to look out at sales for plain horses and ponies that could be made beautiful for his own profit. He saw himself growing rich, moving to a larger house and providing his wife with a parlour maid. But Bob Barton stymied him; for, all at once, the farrier grew disgusted by the work, hated the twitch, the frightened eyes of the horses as he pushed in the ivory skewer, and the dealer's crafty, lucre-loving smile.

When all was said and done, in spite of certain coarse ways, he was a religious man, who thought of animals as "God's beasts".

" 'Tis flying in the face of nature," he announced suddenly, as he cut the fourth hole in a brown gelding's forehead. "God made this young 'oss to be plain, and who am I to know better than the Good Lord!"

He spoke emotionally, as though this sudden feeling of disgust had come as a revelation, and, with his great dark beard and shining eyes, he looked suddenly like an angry prophet. Nothing George could do, say or offer would bring him back to perform the odious operation again. The plain horses stayed plain, the bigger house was never bought, and George's wife continued to lay her own table and open her front door to the few visitors who called.

But the Irish mare prospered and grew sleek and was to be seen on most fine days cantering in the nobleman's park with the pleasant-faced Alice on her back. Her star was greatly admired for the perfection of its shape; and only

four people knew the secret: the dealer, the farrier, the stable boy and the head groom.

But George Ledbetter and Bob Barton were not allowed to forget. Fate, Providence, Divine Retribution – call it what you will – saw to that.

One stormy June evening, some eleven years after the mare was sold, Bob Barton was walking up the hill to the dealer's yard to give advice on a sick horse. Now, his black beard was sprinkled with grey like a dark hedge touched with December frost. His eyes had lost a little of their extraordinary brightness, and his back had a bend in it from all the leaning over horses' hooves as he shod them. Nevertheless, he whistled cheerfully enough, and his strong legs bore his great body well. Above him, the sky was wild with skidding clouds: dark, frilled patches, interspersed with pools of brilliant blue.

"It was June," he thought, "but 'otter than now, when I starred that little bay mare for 'im. What a star that was! What a masterpiece! But 'twas a sin, surely 'twas a sin." And as he thought, he was surprised to see wisps of white vapour, like mist, only a few yards ahead of him.

"More like September than June," he decided, rubbing his eyes with those large, nimble hands. "'Tis to be 'oped it doesn't 'erald rain, or the 'ay will be surely ruined."

But, as he came nearer the mist, it dissolved, and there, right in front of him, was the head of a horse, as though lit by heaven with a halo. A lovely head, delicate, with a fine muzzle and dilated nostrils, and eyes dark as turpentine and bright as polished mahogany, with blue in their centres, like jewels. Right between these magnificent, pleading eyes there shone a snow-white star, more shapely and perfect than any made by nature; a star which Bob Barton recognised with a stab of mingled admiration and remorse, tainted, a moment later, by fear.

"A vision! I've never 'ad a vision. But 'tis the mare. I swear 'tis the mare! The little ears, the eyes – and that look!

My God, forgive us all!"

As these thoughts flashed through the farrier's mind, a trickle of sweat sprang like cold water from his forehead, and a shiver ran down his back like an attack of pins and needles. His swarthy face paled, and, looking down, he saw that his hands were trembling, as though he was possessed of the palsy.

" 'Tis the mare! She's gone and died and come back to haunt us!"

He spoke aloud this time, and there was comfort in hearing his own voice.

"Whoa, my little beauty, steady there. Come on, my little sweet'eart."

His voice was like a caress, so soft and loving that it seemed to stroke, for, as he had grown older, he had come to care deeply for all living things.

He put out one roughly-hewn hand to touch, to feel, but it met nothing but air – air full of the warmth of June and the sweet scent of drying hay. He drew it back then to rub his eyes, and when he looked again the mare had gone. There was nothing but the winding road, climbing up to meet the wild evening sky.

" 'Twas a vision . . . Or it may be I'm getting fancies in my middle years. Worse things 'ave 'appened to men of my age. Could be the Good Lord speaking to me. Could be I've got a screw coming loose in my greying 'ead," he whispered, trying to quell his fear.

He started to walk again and, reasoning with himself, grew calmer. What he feared most was the thought that he might be going mad, that he might end his days in the terrible, over-crowded buildings used as asylums for the insane.

By the time he had reached the dealer's yard he was feeling relaxed and surer of himself. It was a passing freak, a fancy, that was all.

George Ledbetter was leaning against a stable door; his blue eyes had grown more watery with the years, and little

purple veins stood out like threads of dyed cotton on his blob of a nose.

Beside him was another man of around the same age, also with bowed legs, but with a trim figure and a small, bony face.

"Where's the sick 'oss? I've not much time to spare this night," called Bob Barton in his booming voice.

"She's been and died. Colic it was first, a twisted gut – no doubts about that. A sad business. She cost me forty guineas,' replied the dealer. "But it's a blessing you've come, Bob, because there's an 'oss 'ere with a pricked 'oof, and I want the shoe off. Ted 'ere wants 'er, for the young lady who 'ad that Irish mare you put the star on. Well, she's a young mistress now, 'aving married the young Lord

Mountjoy, and she liked that mare so much she said to go to the same place for an 'oss to replace it."

"The mare's dead?" Bob Barton's voice seemed a note higher then usual.

"She was getting long in the tooth," Ted said.

"When did she die?" asked Bob.

"Last Friday, eight days past. She was a beauty, gentle as a kitten, and Miss Alice fair worshipped her."

"You look pale, Bob. Anything the matter? Why, you look as though you've seen a ghost!" exclaimed the dealer. " 'Ere, let me fetch you a chair."

Bob Barton said it was just a passing fit of giddiness, and they should bring the mare out. A bit of work would do him good, and, sure enough, wrenching off the shoe brought the colour back to his face, and he was able to ease the pressure on the wound beneath.

Walking home, he hoped and prayed he would not see the Irish mare again, for now he was sure that it was her ghost which had come to him through the mist.

"The Good Lord rest her soul, if horses have souls," he muttered, making the sign of the cross.

And he never saw her again, although the ghostly sight of her was now lodged for ever in his mind, and often he dreamt of her and woke up shivering and sweating.

George Ledbetter was not so easily spared.

That night in bed, he was disturbed suddenly by his door opening and the sound of unshod hoofs on uneven boards. Sitting up and opening his eyes, he, too, saw the wisps of vapour and, through the vapour, the head of the Irish mare, and those imploring eyes, and he was all at once filled with unexpected remorse for what he had paid Bob Barton to do.

This time, the mare held the hated home-made twitch between her teeth and, rearing up, struck at him with one neat foreleg. He cowered back, his hairy hands hopelessly catching at the air, as though he could seize the twitch and

gain control. He tried to shout, to scream, but his voice seemed to freeze in his throat. Yet he could hear his heart hammering and his breath coming in huge puffs, as if from Bob Barton's bellows down at the Smithy.

He felt no pain at the actual blow from the mare's hoof – just a touch, as though silken thread had passed across his brow. But a moment later a searing pain in his forehead sent him reeling back against the pillows, and his tasselled bedcap (a present from his wife), spun through the air as though thrown by unseen hands, and crashed on the floor as noisily as a saucepan lid falling on bricks.

"A nightmare?" he asked himself in the hoarsest of whispers. But no, his eyes were open and the pain was real. This was no dream; this was reality – or else he was dead and this was hell itself. Had no one else heard the clatter? Was he alone? Except for the mare and that shining white star, that head lit as though by heaven.

"Ellen! Ellen!" He found his voice at last, but it sounded like the wail of a frightened child, rather than the call of a man who owned stables full of horses, and ten acres of land.

And, hearing that cry, the mare swung round on her hocks in one graceful pirouette – and was gone. Where? Through the window? No, the window was half-closed, as before. Through the door? But there was no sound on the wooden staircase. She had gone into nothingness, and so, from nothingness, she could come again. Now there were footsteps – human footsteps.

"Whatever on earth! Whatever next! Shouting at this time of night, when all decent folks are asleep. What's ailing you, a nightmare?"

Ellen was there in her long, white nightgown, a flickering candle in her hand. "You look like death!" she exclaimed. " 'Ere, I'll get you some water." Her grey hair was loose about her shoulders, her bony old feet bare.

"Can't you smell it? – An 'oss 'as been 'ere," said the dealer weakly, scrambling out of bed to retrieve the nightcap. And, indeed, the sweet, pungent smell of horses seemed all about the room.

"Don't be daft, it's them breeches in the chair. The smell never leaves them, does it. It's part of our life, ain't it? 'As been for years."

Ellen fetched a glass of water, scolded him for his fancies and hurried back to the comfort of her feather mattress.

George Ledbetter slept no more that night. At dawn, he rose as usual and saw in the mirror for the first time the purple bump upon his forehead, which was to fester and grow like some hideous boil, so that men shrank from him and averted their gaze, and the local doctors and chemists shook their heads in hopeless puzzlement.

"What could it be, old George Ledbetter's growth? Surely no ordinary infection, no recognisable lump?" people asked, and there was no reply at first, although suspicions were growing in minds, and there was talk in the baker's shop.

In his heart, his poor, meagre heart, which had known and given so little love, the dealer knew whence the lump had come. And Bob Barton knew also, but no one else, for the two men dared not speak for fear of being pronounced mad. Nor did they discuss the matter with each other, not wishing to put such weird and horrible thoughts into words.

In spite of days of irritation, endless poultices and hours of bathing in hot water to draw and soften it, the lump never burst. But in winter, when the first frosts silvered the dark lanes with ice, and the pale sun lay low upon the roof-tops, the swelling started to wrinkle, like an apple kept too long in a barn. And the pain and irritation stopped.

"It's going away," whispered Ellen. "It was like a curse. It 'ad me frightened. But what for? Who would want to put the curse on you, George?"

"I've always been fair and straight," her husband replied, knowing as he spoke that he was uttering a lie.

By Christmas time, the skin was flat again; the scar remained, but began to develop a positive shape, there on the centre of his forehead above the blob of a nose.

After a while, a few local boys called it mockingly "The Star of Bethlehem", and nicknamed the dealer "Bethy". But now the village adults knew better. Many had long been jealous of the dealer's financial successes, feeling them ill-deserved.

"It's one of them 'osses come back to put the mark of a curse upon 'im," some said gladly. "A warning to us all not to ill-treat God's creatures."

For by January the scar had taken its permanent shape. On that crafty forehead there stood out, like some tribal symbol, the perfect, purple outline of a star.

GREEN GRASS OF WYOMING

MARY O'HARA

Carey's filly, Crown Jewels, and a stallion, Thunderhead, are missing. Carey joins the search party that sets out on horseback but she soon finds herself riding alone.

THE WIND DIED DOWN again and the snowflakes that had been drifting through the air seemed to have been sucked up from the earth. It became much colder, and once again the air was crystal clear under the lid of the sky, and far objects seemed near.

As Carey climbed the little peak she realized that no more feathery little stars or gauntlets were falling on her sleeves or face. She kept turning to watch the riders. They progressed in a close pack and a cloud of dust followed them.

When she reached the summit she halted her mare, put the binoculars to her eyes and tried to see if she could pick Ken and Howard out of the group. Then she swung the glasses to right and left, studying every detail of the plains which, because seen through the round circle, took on a starting significance. They seemed not real at all, but something created and planned especially for her.

There slid into view a beautiful picture, framed in the narrow circle: the statue of a horse, pure white, standing on a sharp crest. He was motionless, slightly turned, his head twisted up, every muscle taut and ready.

Carey lowered the binoculars. Her heart was thumping. Was it Thunderhead? No – it wasn't real at all; it was just something in the binoculars –

She sat a moment trying to gather her wits. She looked, without the glasses, at the hill where she had seen the horse but could see nothing new except the barren-looking plains, the ridges and rocks, the Snowy Range far away. No, there it was! A speck of white on a hill-top!

She put the binoculars to her eyes again, seeking him, swinging the glasses in small circles until she captured him. She adjusted the focus with painstaking care until every detail of the stallion was revealed as if in an etching – the intent, white-ringed eyes, the sharply cocked ears, the widely flaring nostrils with a hint of scarlet inside. They palpitated. Was he actually smelling her? Certainly he was watching her – examining her and the mare inch by inch just as she was examining him.

It seemed to Carey that she had never seen anything so beautiful, so wild and so pure.

Then, as she watched, the low sky sank lower. A mist dimmed his shape – he was completely blotted out.

Astonished, she let the glasses fall on their strap and looked around her. Everywhere the sky was sinking. Mist, clouds, fog, snow enveloped her.

She heard a whining in the air. It was in the wind. The snowflakes were not big feathery stars now, but a cutting frozen mist, a horizontal sheet of powdered ice that bit and burned.

She whirled the little roan mare and put heels into her side. "Get back there to camp, and get there in a hurry!" Mamie plunged willingly down the slope.

At the bottom, Carey found she had forgotten just how

she had reached that central, highest peak. On every side there were these steep cones going up. The snow was thicker. She could not hold her eyes open against it. Mamie plodded forward. She seemed to be going up another peak. Carey stopped her and tried to remember. Sitting still on her horse for that moment, she chilled through. Where the wind drove the snow against her leg it melted and instantly froze so that as she tried to brush it off, it was a thin sheet of ice that shattered beneath her hand. And immediately there was another sheet of ice forming on her thigh. Then on her cheek. She kept brushing the ice off. Mamie started forward of her own accord. Carey remembered now that she had gone up and down one small hill before she had reached the central peak. It was this small hill that lay between her and the camp. Mamie was right. They must go up this hill. She urged the little mare forward, bending low, shielding her face and eyes with one arm. She tried to see where she was going but there was only the thick white smother. She thought wonderingly. Why, it's like a sheet wound around me!

They went up the hill and down. Presently Mamie started up another hill. Carey halted her. That's wrong, she thought, there weren't two hills to go up and down. Mamie pulled restlessly at the bit. Carey thought of the wind. It was an easterner, she remembered. The wind was driving from the east. That should direct her to the camp. But here amongst the peaks, the wind was swirling from every direction. You couldn't tell a thing from the wind.

Her teeth were chattering and her body shaking violently. Automatically, she touched her heel to Mamie's side and loosened the reins. The mare plodded forward, up a hill, and Carey didn't know why she let her, for there had not been two hills. It was then she realized that she had no idea where the camp was, and no way of finding it. She was lost.

Mamie plodded part way up the hill, then began to circle it. Carey stopped her again, turned her and forced her to retrace her steps. She was more cold than frightened. She wondered if her face were really freezing as she kept shattering the ice on her cheek and ear. She was glad she had found warm felt gloves in the pocket of the jacket.

The cold drove at her on the whining wind as if it were determined to destroy her. Again, in complete uncertainty, she stopped the mare; Mamie was discouraged and stood with her head hanging. Carey leaned forward and patted her neck and spoke to her, glad to hear the sound of her own voice even though the wind whipped it from her lips. Mamie could hardly have heard it, but still she lifted and turned her head as if comforted.

Everyone knows that horses will find their way home if given their head, thought Carey. But I want to go to the camp. Will she feel that is home because the team and the chuck wagon and the other horse and her master are there? Or will she head for her real home, the Beasley ranch - and how far away is that? She did not remember, but thought it was seven or eight miles. If Mamie had real sense, real horse sense, she would go to the nearest place; she would go to the Monument . . . She gave her her head again, and said, "It's up to you now, Mamie, you find the way."

Mamie went more briskly, in and out the little cones, winding around some, going over others. So chilled that her brain was getting numb, Carey wondered dully if this could really be the way to the camp. Of course, when one is cantering along on the way to a place it doesn't seem any time at all before you're there. Now, fighting back through the blizzard like this, it could seem far, far longer, and still be all right.

But maybe it was wrong. Maybe they were going farther from the camp. Why move at all? Wouldn't it be better just to stay in one spot and wait for Gus or Cookie to come looking for her? But you couldn't stay still. She wondered why no one ever stayed still when they were lost, but wandered on and on.

If she weren't so cold.

She had no idea how far they had gone or how much time had passed. There was nothing to measure by. No change of light. No landmarks to be seen. Just the utter sameness of white driving snow and wind, and the cold getting deeper into her.

Coming out from behind a nill, the wind was behind Mamie and she began a slow trot. She went down a little gulch abruptly, making Carey pitch forward. Up again the other side. In unexpected places there were big drifts of snow already, then a space swept perfectly clean.

Mamie ploughed through some of the drifts, skirted others. Carey knew now that beyond any doubt this was not the way to the camp. They had not crossed any gulches coming. This was more like the badlands. Mamie was going to the Beasley ranch, or she was lost and not going anywhere. Carey decided they must go back and tried to stop the mare. But Mamie fought for her head. When Carey pulled her more determinedly she reared, then plunged. Her foot slipped and she crashed to the earth. Carey rolled free, still holding the reins. But her fingers were stiff and when Mamie scrambled to her feet, one jerk of her head pulled the reins from Carey's hand. In a second, the mare had vanished, and there was no further sight nor sound of her.

Carey sat on the ground a moment, turning her back to the wind, shielding her face, then got to her feet and started forward. It was, she realized, just an aimless wandering. She had not the faintest idea where she was going. But you can't keep still in a storm like that. You'd freeze. Really freeze to death. People did. It was on the front pages of newspapers. Farmers froze to death trying to get from their barns to their houses. Or people caught in automobiles on the highways. You've got to keep your blood circulating. You've got to keep moving . . .

She kept at it a long time, then, worn out, flopped in the lee of a rock on a hillside and told herself she would just rest a minute or two, get a little strength back, and get going again. If only someone would find her now, before she had to move.

It seemed impossible to get going. She tried once, but decided to rest a little longer. Then she did get up. She was shaking all over. She weaved as she walked. She was stiff with the cold. She must sit down again and rest a little longer. Sitting there, her thoughts took a different turn. . . . Perhaps she was not going to be found. Perhaps she was going to be one of those headlines on the front page. "Grandniece of Beaver Greenway lost in the Badlands during a blizzard, frozen to death!" Then she thought of Ken, and hot tears stung her eyes and she had to swallow a lump of self-pity. For this to happen, just after she had met the McLaughlins and all these exciting things had come into her life!

She whipped herself back to reality. A fine thing to do! Just to sit there with her head hanging on her chest, letting herself be frozen to death!

But she could not take another step. Anyway, her only hope was for them to find her. Shout, then! Help them find her! So she opened her mouth to shout and heard the words, "Oh, Ken!" come from her lips and ride away on the wind.

Her head sank on her chest again. She would do it regularly, at intervals, the way a foghorn blows. So, every minute or so, she raised her head and sent the cry of desperation out to the boy who had ridden away to the south-west in search of her filly.

She made herself a little more comfortable where she was crouching in the lee of a rock. There were longer and longer intervals between the calls. She was really getting rested.

She didn't feel so cold. For long minutes she slept profoundly. Then the command she had given herself to call for help, and not to cease calling, flogged her awake again, and she raised her head and cried as loudly as she could, "Oh, Ken!"

Having performed this duty, she smiled happily as her head sank to rest on the arm which was between herself and the earth. She did not wake to cry again.

It was Gus who found her an hour later.

It was if he had known exactly what to expect. He jerked her to her feet, shook her as hard as he could, shouted at her. Her legs collapsed. Her head rolled on her shoulders. Dropping her to the earth, he took a flask out of his pocket, leaned over her, forced some whisky into her mouth and massaged her throat. She choked on the strong liquor. He pulled her to her feet and shook her and jounced her up and down.

No one could know more about the snow sleep than Gus. In Sweden, in the dead of winter, not a month passes but one hears of someone sleeping themselves to death. Not from fatigue. Not from cold. But from a mesmerism that comes from the ceaseless white passes of the snow, binding the will, forbidding effort, bringing peace.

"Und now you git goin'!" thundered Gus, shoving her ahead of him. When she fell, he lifted and shook her and shoved her on again.

She did not whimper. Her eyes flashed open at him now and then; saw a strange, snow-encrusted being who was shouting at her, pushing her and forcing her to wake and walk.

Enough consciousness was roused in her to know what was happening. Agony crept into every limb as her blood began to move again. She must obey him; she must keep going, when she fell, she must get up.

It was a struggle that seemed endless to her, the more she woke and moved, the more pain flowed through all her veins.

Other men joined them before they reached the camp and she was aware of the riders coming galloping in, horses and men so coated in snow that they were unrecognizable. There was much shouting. Gus lifted her and put her into the cab of the truck which was warm because the engine was going and the heater was on. Gus left the door open and stood outside, talking to the men. Cookie had harnessed the chuck wagon.

She could hear what they were shouting - to make for

Beasley's ranch. Cookie knew every turn of the country and could lead the way - a safe way for the truck to follow, and the station wagon and pick-up, and the men on their horses since it was impossible to load them into the truck. Some of the men shouted that they would make for home.

Suddenly Gus slammed the door shut and she was alone in the cab. The feeling of comfort and security was almost too much for her, and again her eyes were hot with tears. She stuck her fists into them. Her body still felt queer.

The door opened and Gus put Ken into the cab beside her. "Keep her movin' and talkin', Ken, shake her if you have to, I'll be back."

Ken's face was both awed and frightened. He took her hands and rubbed them as if he feared they would break. She tried to smile at him.

The other door opened, Gus climbed in, speeded up the engine, opened the window to stick his head out and shout some last orders, then the truck was under way. Gus closed the window, without a word handed the flask to Ken and told him to make Carey get some more down her.

Carey obediently gulped the strong stuff, Gus looked down into her eyes searchingly and said, as the truck lurched on, "You be all right now, Carey."

Carey nodded at him but still did not speak until she turned back to Ken and suddenly said. "Oh, Ken, I called you and called you and called you!"

"Gosh, Carey!" Ken mumbled helplessly as he fastened the top of the flask and handed it back to Gus.

"Ken! I saw Thunderbird!"

The boy stared at her, wondering if this was part of her snow-sleep dream.

"I really saw him, through the binoculars, standing way off on a crest, like a white statue, just what you said."

For a long moment their eyes met, sharing all that had happened, for Carey's mind had gone all of the way towards death – the rest would have been easy – and her eyes clung to Ken's and she leaned towards him, putting the burden of this on him too, to help her carry it, and suddenly the long-held tears and sobs burst through and she cried, "Oh, Ken!' and flung herself on his breast. He put his arm around her and held her tight.

The cars carried no lights. They followed one behind the other close after the chuckwagon. It was the team in the chuckwagon that led the way, knowing it well, going and their backs hunched slightly, heading for home.

Gus glanced sideways at Ken and Carey and said with a little grin, "Looks more like huggin' dan shakin' – vell – so long as she don' go to sleep again."

Fifteen minutes before the little cavalcade turned into the Beasley ranch, Mamie trotted up to the bunkhouse, her reins dragging. She stopped before the lighted windows and gave a beseeching whinny.

THE MIDWINTER
GOLD CUP

DICK FRANCIS

from Nerve

I WATCHED THE starter's hand. He had a habit of
stretching his finger just before he pulled the lever to
let the tapes up, and I had no intention of letting
anyone get away before me and cut me out of the position I
had acquired on the rails.

The starter stretched his fingers. I kicked Template's
flanks. He was moving quite fast when we went under the
rising tapes, with me lying flat along his withers to avoid
being swept off, like other riders who had jumped the start
too effectively in the past. The tapes whistled over my head
and we were away, securely on the rails on the inside curve
for at least the next two miles.

The first three fences were the worst, as far as my
comfort was concerned. By this time we had jumped the
fourth – the water – I had felt the thinly healed crusts on
my back tear open, had thought my arms and shoulders
would split apart with the strain of controlling Template's
eagerness, had found just how much my wrists and hands
had to stand from the tug of the reins.

My chief feeling, as we landed over the water, was one of

relief. It was all bearable; I could contain it and ignore it, and get on with the job.

The pattern of the race was simple from my point of view, because from start to finish I saw only three other horses, Emerald and the two lightly-weighted animals whom I had allowed to go on and set the pace. The jockeys of this pair, racing ahead of me nose for nose, consistently left a two-foot gap between themselves and the rails, and I reckoned that if they were still there by the time we reached the second last fence in the straight, they would veer slightly towards the stands, as horses usually do at Ascot, and widen the gap enough for me to get through.

My main task until then was keeping Emerald from cutting across to the rails in front of me and being able to take the opening instead of Template. I left just too little room between me and the front pair for Emerald to get in, forcing the mare to race all the way on my outside. It didn't matter that she was two or three feet in front: I could see her better there, and Template was too clever a jumper to be brought down by the half-length trick – riding into a fence half a length in front of an opponent, causing him to take off at the same moment as oneself and land on top of the fence instead of safely on the ground the other side.

With the order unchanged we completed the whole of the first circuit and swept out to the country again. Template jumped the four fences down to Swinley Bottom so brilliantly that I kept finding myself crowding the tails of the pacemakers as we landed, and had to ease him back on the flat each time to avoid taking the lead too soon, and yet not ease him so much that Emerald could squeeze into the space between us.

From time to time I caught a glimpse of the grimness on Emerald's jockey's face. He knew perfectly well what I was doing to him, and if I hadn't beaten him to the rails and made a flying start, he would have done the same to me.

For another half-mile the two horses in front kept going splendidly, but one of the jockeys picked up his whip at the third last fence, and the other was already busy with his hands. They were dead ducks, and because of that they swung a little wide going round the last bend into the straight. The Irishman must have had his usual bend tactics too fixed in his mind, for he chose that exact moment to go to the front. It was not a good occasion for that manoeuvre. I saw him spurt forward from beside me and accelerate, but he had to go round on the outside of the two front horses who were themselves swinging wide, and he was wasting lengths in the process. The mare carried seven pounds less weight than Template, and on that bend she lost the advantage they should have given her.

After the bend, tackling the straight for the last time, with the second last fence just ahead, Emerald was in the lead on the outside, then the two tiring horses, then me.

There was a three foot gap then between the innermost pacemaker and the rails. I squeezed Template. He pricked his ears and bunched his colossal muscles and thrust himself forward into the narrow opening. He took off at the second last fence half a length behind and landed a length in front of the tiring horse, jumping so close to him on one side and to the wings on the other that I heard the other jockey cry out in surprise as I passed.

One of Template's great advantages was his speed away from a fence. With no check in his stride he sped smoothly on still hugging the rails, with Emerald only a length in front on our left. I urged him a fraction forward to prevent the mare from swinging over to the rails and blocking me at the last fence. She needed two lengths' lead to do it safely, and I had no intention of letting her have it.

The utter joy of riding Template lay in the feeling of immense power which he generated. There was no need to make the best of things, on his back; to fiddle and scramble, and hope for others to blunder, and find nothing to spare for a finish. He had enough reserve strength for his jockey to be able to carve up the race as he wished, and there was nothing in racing, I thought, more ecstatic than that.

I knew, as we galloped towards the last fence, that Template would beat Emerald if he jumped it in anything like his usual style. She was a length ahead and showing no sign of flagging, but I was still holding Template on a tight rein. Ten yards from the fence, I let him go. I kicked his flanks and squeezed with the calves of my legs and he went over the birch like an angel, smooth, surging, the nearest to flying one can get.

He gained nearly half a length on the mare, but she didn't give up easily. I sat down and rode Template for my life, and he stretched himself into his flat-looking stride. He came level with Emerald half-way along the run in. She hung on grimly for a short distance, but Template would have none of it. He floated past her with an incredible increase of speed, and he won, in the end, by two clear lengths.

There are times beyond words, and that was one of them. I patted Template's sweating neck over and over. I could have kissed him. I would have given him anything. How does one thank a horse? How could one ever repay him, in terms he would understand, for giving one such a victory?

BILLY MOSBY'S
NIGHT RIDE

A New England legend retold by

ROBERT D. SAN SOUCI

I N THE EARLY 1800s, in a small town in a remote part of New York state, a young boy named Billy Mosby, whose parents had died, was raised by his grandparents, Enoch and Anne Mosby.

Billy helped out on his grandparents' farm, getting up early to milk the cows and feed the pigs and gather the eggs. Though he sometimes grumbled when his grandfather rousted him out of bed before sunrise, he liked his new life and found little to complain about.

He was afraid, however, of his grandparents' neighbour, Francis Woolcott, who lived a half a mile down the road from them. Every afternoon, when the sun was westering and long shadows had begun to creep down the hillsides, Billy would watch from a window as Francis Woolcott, like a tall, dark shadow, strode down the dusty road towards the grove of ash and chestnut trees at the end of the road.

He lived in a cabin, which he had let fall nearly to ruin. But he never wanted for anything. The farmers whispered that he was a witch – and feared him so much that they gave him pork, flour, meal, cider, or anything that he might

215

need. If they didn't, neighbours said, he would make a horse come to a dead halt in the middle of ploughing, or make a man run around, flapping his folded arms like wings and clucking like a chicken. But even worse, rumour said, was the fact that the old man could conjure up thirteen night riders – demons straight from hell – when the moon was growing old. They would go anywhere he told them to, and do all sorts of mischief. Whenever he heard about the demon riders, Billy felt a thrill of fear – and an eagerness to see these creatures of the night (from a safe distance, of course.)

Woolcott never bothered Billy's grandparents. They were polite to the man when they met him in the lane, and thought the talk of witchery was so much foolishness. "Good Christian folk should be about their business and not wasting time scaring each other with such nonsense," declared Anne Mosby.

But Billy kept an open mind; there was so much talk in the neighbourhood, he couldn't believe *everybody* was wrong. He kept his thoughts to himself, however: he knew there was no arguing with his grandparents once their minds were made up.

But Billy's curiosity about Francis Woolcott grew the more he tried not to think about the strange old man.

"I've got to see for myself," he decided one evening. So after his grandparents were asleep in their room, he slipped out of his bedroom window and ran down the road to Woolcott's cabin. A three-quarter moon overhead gave plenty of light to see by.

But when he was near the dark cabin, Billy saw the old man open the front door. The boy ducked behind a bush; but, peeking from behind some leaves, he saw that Woolcott was carrying bundles of oat straw in his arms. With a quick glance up and down the road, the shadowy figure headed towards the grove of ash and chestnut trees at the end of the lane.

When it seemed safe, Billy followed. Something told him that tonight he would find out the truth about Woolcott's witchery.

The man went directly to a clearing in the centre of the grove. There he carefully laid out thirteen bundles of oat straw in a circle. Standing inside this ring, Woolcott extended his arms and began to turn, muttering words that Billy, watching around the trunk of a chestnut tree, could not hear.

As the witch spun faster, the bundles of oat straw began to put off sprouts so they looked as if they were growing into gnarly plants. But the "roots" quickly became horses' legs, the bundles themselves became the bodies of sleek black horses, and the strange "blossoms" became their heads and tails.

Then a cloud passed across the moon, and the clearing was suddenly dark. When the moonlight returned, Billy saw that there was now a rider on the back of each horse. They were wrapped in black cloaks and had their broad-brimmed hats drawn down so that the boy could see nothing of their faces.

Quickly Francis Woolcott began giving instructions to these mysterious horsemen, sending them off in different directions. Sometimes a night rider would go alone; sometimes two would gallop off together. When all but one had been sent away, Billy, leaning closer to try and hear what Woolcott was saying, stepped on a dry, fallen branch that gave a loud SNAP!

Instantly the man at the centre of the clearing came bounding across and grabbed the boy before he could run. Woolcott's hand was like a claw on Billy's shoulder as he hauled the boy into the clearing, where the last night rider silently waited.

"Please don't hurt me!" begged Billy. "I promise I won't tell."

"Tell whomever you please," said the man. "It doesn't .natter a jot to me." Then he fixed Billy with a thoughtful stare and stroked his chin. "It might just be I could use a brave lad like you as an apprentice. You've got curiosity enough to kill a cat nine times over. And you seem bright enough." Now Woolcott was rubbing his hands together eagerly. "Yes, you have all the makings of a fine apprentice. So we'll begin your lessons tonight: since you were curious about my friend, ride with him awhile – satisfy your curiosity."

Before Billy could even ask what an "apprentice" was, the old man picked him up with surprising strength and swung him into the saddle, behind the shadowy rider. "Now go!" the old man yelled.

Without a word, the rider urged his midnight steed to a trot and guided the animal out of the clearing to the road. Billy found he was stuck to the sleek, black horse as though he were a part of it. He glanced once over his shoulder and saw Francis Woolcott standing in the clearing, watching him. The rider in front said nothing; but Billy felt him urging his horse to a gallop, the moment they were free of the trees.

In uncanny silence they rushed down the lane. The silky black cloak of the man in front of him whipped back around Billy, obscuring his view much of the time. The horses' hooves made no sound on the rock-strewn roadway; the only sound was the wind rushing past the boy's ears. They raced like hurricanes across fields and through woods – leaping bushes, fences, even trees without effort.

Billy lost all track of time and distance. He began to think they were going to ride forever, when they reached the gates of a farm Billy had never seen before. The house was quiet and dark.

Reining in his horse in front of the barn, the night rider cried:

"Tangle the horses' tails this night;

Let the hogs all sing and dance upright."

The doors of the barn flew open, and two horses charged into the yard. They whinnied in terror, and Billy could see their tails were so twisted together that they began running in a circle, which only frightened them more. Behind them, in the shadows of the barn, he saw the nightmarish forms of three pigs, squealing and prancing around on their hind legs, as though they were trying to sing and dance.

Lamps were lit in the farmhouse; Billy could hear shouts. The night rider wheeled his horse and galloped away from the farm. They travelled fast as a whirlwind through unfamiliar countryside. Long after the moon had set, Billy began to recognize landmarks. In the starlight he saw that they were nearing the cluster of chestnut and ash trees where his adventure had begun.

But at the very edge of the grove, Billy's rider suddenly vanished; the black horse turned into a bundle of oat straw under him, and he tumbled to the ground with a thump.

He lay for a long time, just catching his breath. Then he got to his feet, grabbed the bundle of oat straw, and ran to tell his grandparents what he had seen. Before he reached home, he looked at the oat straw and thought, "They'll never believe me." So he crept quietly back into bed and said nothing, though in his mind he relived the amazing night ride again and again.

The next evening, sitting at the kitchen table helping his grandmother shell peas, Billy asked, "What's an 'apprentice'?"

"A beginner, a learner," Anne Mosby answered, "a boy who works for someone so he can learn the man's trade." She looked at her grandson curiously. "You thinking of hiring yourself out to someone?"

"No," said Billy, "I just heard the word somewhere, and I wondered what it meant."

But as he worked at the peas, his mind began to race. He imagined what it might be like to wave his hands and have pigs dance in the moonlight or bundles of oat straw turn into night riders on magical horses. If he could ever get up the nerve, he thought, he might, just *might*, ask Francis Woolcott to make him an apprentice. It was a frightening thought, but it was also an exciting one.

But there were no more stories of the thirteen night riders after that. Though Billy eagerly watched the road past the farm, old Francis Woolcott, who was ninety years old, no longer visited the neighbours and took away the farmers' goods with him. The boy heard several people mutter, "He's died or gone to the devil, and not a moment too soon."

No one would go near the silent, tumble-down cabin. When Billy suggested he and his grandparents should take a look, Anne and Enoch told him to mind his own business.

When his need to know what had happened and his fear that he might never learn the secrets of night riding got the better of him, Billy slipped away one afternoon to the little house that looked completely deserted. He knocked several times; when a faint cry came from inside, the boy pushed open the door.

The cramped room inside smelt stale and sour. Old Francis Woolcott lay under a pile of filthy bedclothes on a cot in one corner. At first Billy thought the old man was dead, his eyes were closed so tight. But they popped open, and Woolcott asked sharply, "What are you doing here, boy?"

"I ... well ... ," Billy mumbled.

"Speak up!" Francis Woolcott demanded.

"I want to become your apprentice," the boy managed to get out.

"Then you're a fool, boy," said the old man bitterly. "Why would you want to learn such things?"

"I want to call up night riders of my own," Billy said eagerly. "I want to be able to turn people I don't like into chickens."

"There's a price on such secrets, boy," whispered the old

man, suddenly turning his head to watch the door. "There's a terrible price which nobody should have to pay. But I'm going to, soon enough."

"What do you mean?" asked Billy, wondering if maybe the old man had gone out of his head.

"*He's* coming for me soon," croaked Francis Woolcott. "I'm dying, but I won't have any peace."

"Maybe I'd better go get my grandfather," said Billy, frightened by the other's fear. He turned to go, but the old man grabbed his wrist with a clutch like a circle of iron.

Billy heard a sudden clap of thunder, unexpected on what had been a pleasant summer day. Staring out the window, he saw rain pelting down from a sudden storm. In the shadows, the dying man's face had such a horrible look that Billy gave a small cry of alarm. With each peal of thunder, Woolcott trembled more and more.

"*He's* coming," the old man said again, struggling to sit up in bed. Then he gave a cry and fell back on his pillow.

Billy heard the loudest crash of thunder yet. Then, over the sound of the wind and rain, he heard galloping hooves in the road. They stopped just outside the cabin.

Francis Woolcott, terror-stricken, tightened his hold on the boy, and tried to say something that Billy couldn't make out. The door was flung open, and a night rider stood like a monstrous shadow in the doorway. The old man gave a final, strangulated cry, then let his hand drop limply away from Billy's wrist.

There was a flash of lightning; for an instant Billy caught a glimpse of the rider's face. He saw horns, skin the colour of raw beef, and eyes that burned like coals. The room smelt of sulphur and the sound of rain on the roof was deafening. Then the figure strode to the bed, picked up the old man as if he weighed no more than a bundle of oat straw, and carried him through the door.

The panel slammed behind them. There was a peal of thunder, then the sound of galloping hooves disappearing into the rain.

But when Billy had calmed down enough to leave the cabin that now held only him, he found the road outside was dry. At home he found his grandparents hadn't noticed any rain or heard any thunder. When he tried to tell them what he had seen, they scolded him for making up outlandish stories.

Later Anne asked her grandson, "You still thinking about becoming someone's apprentice?"

"No, ma'am," said Billy, "not now, not *ever!*"

ACKNOWLEDGEMENTS

The publisher would like to thank the copyright holders for permission to reproduce the following copyright material:

Enid Bagnold: Reed Consumer Books Ltd for the extract from *National Velvet* by Enid Bagnold, William Heinemann Ltd 1935. Copyright © Enid Bagnold 1935. Daphne du Maurier: Curtis Brown Ltd, London on behalf of the Chichester Partnership for the extract from *Jamaica Inn* by Daphne du Maurier. Copyright © Daphne du Maurier Browning 1936. Walter Farley: Hodder & Stoughton Publishers Ltd for "The Sentinel" from *The Black Stallion Revolts* by Walter Farley. Dick Francis: Michael Joseph Ltd for "The Midwinter Gold Cup" (an abridged version), first printed in *Best Racing and Chasing Stories Two*, Faber & Faber Ltd 1969, taken from *Nerve* by Dick Francis, Michael Joseph 1964. Copyright © Dick Francis 1964. Marguerite Henry: Simon & Schuster Books for Young Readers, an imprint of Simon & Schuster Children's Publishing Division, for "The Birth of the King" from *The King of the Wind* by Marguerite Henry. Copyright © Marguerite Henry 1948, renewed 1976. Patricia Leitch: D.J. Murphy Publishers Ltd for "Midnight Stallion" by Patricia Leitch from Pony Tales. Copyright © D.J. Publishers Ltd 1988. C.S. Lewis: HarperCollins Publishers Ltd for the extract from *The Magician's Nephew* by C.S. Lewis. Copyright © C.S. Lewis 1955. Elyne Mitchell: Curtis Brown Ltd, London for "Golden the Beautiful" from *The Silver Brumby* by Elyne Mitchell, Hutchinson. Copyright © Elyne Mitchell 1958. Mary O'Hara: Laurence Pollinger Ltd and the Estate of Mary O'Hara for the extract from *Green Grass of Wyoming* by Mary O'Hara, Methuen. Copyright © Mary O'Hara 1946. George Orwell: A.M. Heath & Co. Ltd for the extract from *Animal Farm* by George Orwell. Copyright © The Estate of the late Sonia Brownwell Orwell and Martin Secker & Warburg Ltd. K.M. Peyton: Oxford University Press for "A Ride with Mark" from *Flambards* by K.M. Peyton, OUP 1967. Copyright © K.M. Peyton 1967. Christine Pullein-Thompson: Jennifer Luithlen Agency for the extract from *Phantom Horse Comes Home* by Christine Pullein-Thompson. Copyright © Christine Pullein-Thompson 1970. Diana Pullein-Thompson: Jennifer Luithlen Agency for "A Star for a Lady" by Diana Pullein-Thompson. Copyright © Diana Pullein-Thompson. Gerald Raftery: William Morrow & Co. Inc. for the extract from *Snow Cloud Stallion* by Gerald Raftery. Copyright © Gerald Raftery 1953. Arthur Ransome: Random House UK Ltd and the Estate of the author for "The Firebird, the Horse of Power and the Princess Vasilissa" from *Old Peter's Russian Tales* by Arthur Ransome, Jonathan Cape. Copyright © Arthur Ransome 1916. Sinclair Ross: McClelland & Stewart, Toronto for "The Outlaw" from *The Lamp at Noon and Other Stories* by Sinclair Ross. Copyright © Sinclair Ross. Robert D. San Souci: Doubleday, a division of Bantam Doubleday Dell Publishing Group, Inc. for "Bill Mosby's Night Ride" from *Short and Shivery: Thirty Chilling Tales* by Robert D. San Souci. Copyright © Robert D. San Souci 1987. A.F. Tschiffely: John Johnson Ltd on behalf of the Estate for "A Gaucho in the Pampa" by A.F. Tschiffely from *My First Horse*, Lunn. Copyright © The Estate of A.F. Tschiffely 1947.

Every effort has been made to obtain permission to reproduce copyright material but there may be cases where we have been unable to trace a copyright holder. The publisher will be happy to correct any omissions in future printings.